We had gone to the impersonal bed, with its coolness and blankness. I could feel her still trembling. Her slip was white, with lace where it contained her breasts. The lace and the nylon were very white; with an odd digression of the mind at a time when one hardly thinks I remembered something she had said, amused, about being told at school that what one wore under one's dress was of greater importance than the dress.

She said, " 'At last, at last, or some such rot.' " The words broke in the middle, as if she had swallowed because her mouth was dry.

I knew I had read the words somewhere or heard them, perhaps in a film, but I didn't know where, or try to place them.

"Judith."

"Oh, darling."

I think her passion surprised me; it had in it a quality of *gladness*, I think it was, that a little surprised me.

The afternoon darkened, and the rain with it.

She almost slept.

The Other Side of Venus

by
Shirley Verel

The Naiad Press Inc.
1988

Printed in the United States of America
First Naiad Press Edition

Cover design by The Women's Graphic Center
Typesetting by Sandi Stancil

ISBN: 0-941483-07-X

TO RAY
With all my love

Part One

I

It isn't the kind of story one would choose to tell. At any rate I can't imagine that. If secrecy had been possible I would have chosen secrecy. But now I think I shall be almost thankful for the chance to tell it. To tell all of it. To say, at least : this, not that, is what it was like. This is what happened. This is the truth.

I first saw Diana the day I went to collect the Austin Healey I had on order. It had been on order since well before Christmas, but I had put off collecting it. Then Martin had offered to drive it through the rush-hour for me. I was Martin's wife and am still called ' Mrs. Allart '—which always seems strange to me. He made the offer when he telephoned my office about a mortgage for his brother, who was buying a house. We had met sometimes since our divorce. There was no overt ill-feeling left between us. So far as I was concerned there was no ill-feeling of any sort. I knew that I was to blame, anyway, for the one impossible thing that had wrecked our marriage. As for him, whatever he felt, there would have seemed no point to him in cherishing animosity for its own sake. But all the same it was the first time he had gone out of his way to see me.

High Holborn at five o'clock might have been a lane, for all it worried him. He sat solid and casual in the driver's seat, one hand half the time on his knee. I enjoyed his easy confidence as a driver, and what had become for me the luxury of not having to do the worrying

3

myself. I suppose I enjoyed feeling, however briefly, that he was between me and the traffic : or the world. The nature of my relationship with him having once been what it had, I could still feel this.

Every now and then he glanced at me as we talked, and instead of the bluntly-made, masculine profile I saw the whole of his face. In a sense it was like seeing the whole of him as a man. He looked what he was. His eyes looked intelligent, and something else—something suggesting a quality not so much of sensitiveness as selectiveness, the faculty of distinguishing between things at unobvious levels. There was humour in his face without this being the dominant expression. His mouth was full and well-shaped. Where there were lines they cut deep into the brown skin.

Being with him had the familiarity of a house one has lived in for years. Only it was as if some of the doors were locked now, and all the floors had been newly carpeted. We walked about thinking what we were doing. There was no longer any danger that either of us would stumble or slip.

" Do you want to go straight home ? " he asked.

" I'm having dinner with Andrew. He's invited Ammersgate for the evening."

" Oh." In the pause he lit a cigarette. " How *is* Ammersgate these days ? "

" Getting better. Not that I've seen him. But Andrew says he's all right. He's taking things quietly."

" I didn't know they were friends, especially."

" It's really more a question, I should imagine, of the number of friends Ammersgate has with money to invest, and the fun he still seems to get out of persuading them to invest it. Though it's true he has something of a passion for the personal relationship."

" Oh, I see."

At one end of our separation, I thought, had been the beating heart, the exhaustion, the secretly trembling legs ; all the bitter emotional business of deciding to part. At the other now was deliberate civility.

He smoked his cigarette.

When we had lived together the things connected with his smoking had been permanently all over the place. Pipes, matches, packets of cigarettes, ash. Our rooms in the morning had smelt of cold smoke. It was a curious thing to have missed ; but I had missed it. I think it had stood afterwards for living intimately with somebody. My own flat, where I lived alone, and nobody smoked, had seemed empty and sad.

He said, " Do you find living alone makes you go out practically anywhere rather than stay at home ? "

" This week Helen's at the flat."

" I'll take you to Westhaw. I can get a train back. That wasn't an answer."

" It's too far." He disregarded the objection, and we drove on. " I suppose I find home is where my job is the least satisfying."

" I never suspected you of being altogether a career woman. If there is such a thing."

" But what is the other thing ? You never suspected me of being very good at love."

" With me." He half smiled. " There are other men."

I didn't answer.

" Love isn't a luxury. Is it? It's a necessity. Most people can't just take it or leave it alone. For women even marriage might be a necessity."

" And for men? "

" Men can make do on less. Or on different. If you mean me, ' I grow old, I grow old '—and out of falling in love. So I don't get as far as proposing."

It was by chance the quotation was a hackneyed one. He read a great deal, and Eliot was a poet he knew well. He had said once he loved the words without subscribing to the philosophy. I remembered when. It was just before we were married. We had come on a picnic. I disliked picnics, but this one had been better than most because of a hot and invariable sun. I was lying in the sun beyond the rim of shade from some trees where we had picnicked, whilst he sat well back into the shade : his shirt off, passive, lazy in the heat, his voice soft, talking about whatever came into his head. The occasion had been important to me because of the feeling I had had suddenly of being in a state of intimacy and harmony with him, of being something near to happy.

" Not that you would know about that," he added now.

" About falling in love? "

" About the corroding thirties. I find they begin to lose the knack of personal passion. The function of such an extravagance in human affairs, of course, is just to force one's hand ; promote the offering of ' all '."

" So we do it best—fall in love—when we most want our hand forced? "

" Or worst," he said, and laughed.

6

We began to leave London behind.

He had never driven a Healey until that evening. After a little while he said, "It's a nice car. Not that I can think what you want with it. In December."

"I feel like going fast."

"Well, that, anyway, shouldn't be difficult. When it's run in, don't forget."

At Westhaw he suggested a drink. We drank Manzanilla sherries. I had got my taste for them from him. He asked me if I remembered saying they were like drinking sea-fever. I didn't remember but thought, if I had said it, it was apt.

When we had finished, and were standing outside the pub, he said, "Don't kill yourself," patting the car's cream bonnet. "If you don't, might we see something of each other occasionally? After all, it was never as friends we couldn't get along."

Our good-byes over, he pulled at the belt of his raincoat, and walked away—thick-set, dark, thirty-seven. He disappeared into the station. It would take him perhaps fifty minutes to get back to London.

Too late to do anything about it, I noticed he had forgotten his gloves.

I had married him in good faith. Though I had wanted what I imagined he could give me, it wasn't to have been at his expense. But I had made a bad mistake in ever supposing resolution any guarantee of success. It's no guarantee. One can resolve to one's heart's content, for instance, about a body that won't co-operate. In time disharmony had been everywhere, sailing under any colours.

7

People are mostly in no hurry either to fail themselves, or to hurt other people. We didn't hurry to admit our marriage was a failure. But when finally the truth began to spill over, in a savage kind of a way it seemed almost a relief.

We had been to a lecture at the university. Martin lectured in law. All I recollect about the lecture is that it was given by an American woman who called herself 'Mary' as if she had no other name. Afterwards we sat about and had 'refreshments'. I had only come to please him, and now he seemed to have forgotten I was there.

As we drove home I was silent, wanting him to talk to me, to make the first move. But he didn't.

It was terribly cold. When we got in I went straight to our bedroom and sat down on the floor by the electric fire. He glanced at me, but didn't say anything. It was suddenly as if we had quarrelled, though nothing had been said. I heard him moving about in the kitchen. After a minute or two I went out to him. He was making tea.

" This is really the wife's job."

It had enough of an edge to it to place it as not a pleasantry.

" I would have made some tea ; but I don't see why it is, especially." I hadn't been at home all day any more than he had, and one is filled at such times with a passion for justice.

" I drove us home."

" Only because you'd rather."

" Well, don't let's argue about it." He poured water

8

into the tea-pot. " All the same, I should have thought most wives would have been glad to make the gesture."

That was getting near.

" I'm sorry I'm such an unsatisfactory wife."

He said, not looking up from the tea-pot, " So am I. We won't go into it."

" Hadn't we better, after that ? "

" It doesn't matter."

" What are you so sorry about ? "

" If you insist," he said, and for the first time he looked at me, " I'm sorry to have a wife who doesn't want me. I'm sorry that when I kiss you I can feel you cross your fingers it won't lead to anything worse. That when we're in bed you keep your back turned for fear I should start anything. I'm sorry to be put up with. Though I don't think you know what it is to want a man. Or if you do, it isn't me."

In the silence I could hear the water in the kettle gently dying away.

" Martin——"

But what, after all, does one say to explain to one's husband that the only pleasure one can know with him is no more than some sort of physical spasm : unnatural, empty and meaningless in itself, having nothing to do with sex.

" Other women aren't like it."

Then I wanted to say, because something in his voice had intensified my feelings of guilt, and of helplessness, ' Why don't you get what you want from other women ? '

But I couldn't say that to him, either.

I don't know whether he did or not, while we were

9

together. I still don't know. There are some things in a marriage, they might be anything, it always remains impossible to talk about. Intimacy creates barriers as well as removes them. But there was the girl at a party Lawrence, one of our directors, gave. She was very young, perhaps seventeen ; very pretty and very flirtatious. I suppose if I hadn't gone to get my bag from the bedroom at just the moment when I did I shouldn't have known that Martin had kissed her. Or perhaps I should have known. If not about her, then about someone else. It's strange how things come out : somehow or other, sooner or later. He had a tinge of lipstick on his mouth. It made him look slightly indecent. We were all very light and civilised ; after all, it was a party. But I knew then it was hopeless, the situation was hopeless. For what I had felt was less jealousy than it was envy.

He apologised later. He said, " You know, it was only a kiss."

But it wasn't long afterwards we decided to separate.

I said I was sorry. I hated the idea of going into the truth with him, and it didn't seem at the time it could help much, or make much real difference.

I didn't leave him because I expected to be any happier. I don't think I expected anything. I felt curiously neutral now about what would happen. I think I felt that whatever happened, either way, it could only be for the worst. I left him because I thought it was the least I could do.

I would rather—that evening going to Westhaw—he had told me he had fallen in love again than that he hadn't.

10

My way from Westhaw station was along quiet lanes.
I was glad of this when I came to drive. Four or five
years ago Andrew Jefferson, the chairman of our board
since my father died, had seen a house called ' Four
Winds ' on the top of Westhaw Hill, and wanted it. It
was a grey stone house, less big than imposing. I was
never quite sure if it was beautiful. Andrew thought it
was. His mother, on the other hand—she had been
living with him—had disliked it for ' looking like an oast
house ', and disliked the idea of living at the top of a
steep hill even more, being eighty. He was fond of his
mother, but he was going to have the house—so she went
to live with her married son in Truro, and he lived alone.
Or that was what he had been doing, until a week or
so ago.

The wooded grounds now looked bare ; in Spring they
were littered thick with daffodils.

I was approaching the gates when I became aware of
a car behind me.

I turned into the drive, and stalled the engine, and
couldn't get the car to start again. The other car waited,
its engine ticking over. The murmured conversation of
its occupants just reached me through the darkness. A
girl laughed, got out of the car and came towards me.
She said, still with the remains of laughter in her voice,
" Excuse me, but you haven't got the hand-brake on,
have you ? "

" I don't have, as a rule."

As she stood at my window I had a quick impression
of somebody young, of excitement, of a smartness experi-
mental, hit-and-miss. She had dark hair, which was

11

almost straight, at any rate without curls, and had been well cut.

Just for an instant she returned my look, then her expression changed ; some of the excitement seemed to die out of it. " I'm not being very helpful," she said briefly. " I'll make Gerry drive round the block or something." And before I could say anything further she turned and went back to her car.

Left to myself, I drove without difficulty to the front door, wondering if it had been Diana.

Andrew answered my knock.

2

Andrew was just on fifty-five. He was short and getting if not fat then heavy, but his suits and shirts were so good and so professionally well cared for that he very nearly suggested elegance ; certainly wealth. His face was sallow, and his hair completely black. Not that there was any secret about his hair. The bottle was there to see for anyone going into his bathroom who chanced to notice it. His features were rather big and fleshy. In some ways he looked a bit like a political caricature of a business man. He was, I suppose, rather ugly if you thought about it, which I hadn't done for years, but it wasn't the kind of ugliness that mattered. You didn't have to overcome it first. On the contrary, there was something almost satisfying about his appearance. It was consistent somehow ; it all fitted in. To

12

one side of his mouth he had a gold tooth which showed when he smiled.

He smiled now, and welcomed me with the conventional affabilities of a board-room greeting.

Our relations were cordial without being those of personal friends. Though I visited his home quite often it was invariably a matter of mixing pleasure with business.

His home was luxurious, and incredibly well run. He had an excellent French cook. He was, in fact, looked after by the best professionals money could buy. In many respects his home was more like a luxurious club than a home, and he seemed to use it more like a club— rather impersonally, for his own advantage. To set himself off as a successful man.

We conversed a moment in the hall.

A friend of his in shipping whose views he respected had told him once that carpets and mirrors made a room, so he had them ; he uncompromisingly had them.

He even had small weighing-machines in all the bedrooms. It might have seemed ludicrous but somehow, when one knew Andrew, it only seemed typical.

Anything he could use that money could buy I think he liked to show that he could buy. If there are things it can't buy, those were the things he had given little sign of wanting in the years I had known him.

He took me into Ammersgate then.

" Here he is," he said. " Doesn't look bad for a crock, does he ? These sons of bishops are a tough lot."

I hadn't seen Ammersgate since he had had his thrombosis and resigned from our board. He advanced upon me solicitously. " I'm really getting quite well ; but, Judith, my dear," he said in his high, gentle voice, " you look . . ." He paused. For an unhappy moment I wondered if he was actually going to say ' older '. But he said, " tired."

Andrew stood looking at him with the complex look which arises from looking at two things at once : in this case a man and his usefulness.

He was slender, and didn't fill out his suit or his warm, caramel-coloured waistcoat. He had a bony, delicate face, and blue-veined hands like a thin woman's.

I didn't sympathise with Andrew's fundamental contempt of the man. I have always thought, for as long as I have thought of such things at all, that any passion for the pure male or the pure female, like a passion for racial purity, is as hopeless as it is silly. Human beings may have, will have, human preferences. There it is. But judgment in such a context must surely be irrational.

" Have you been over-working ? " he asked.

" These double-dyed career women—they're all the same. Keep at it." Andrew laughed, then looked at his watch. " That's something, anyway, you can't say about Diana. Where have they got to, by the way ? They're supposed to be coming in for drinks. Before they're off out again somewhere or other."

He had already told me his niece was staying at ' Four Winds '.

Ammersgate went gossipily into this at the first opportunity he had. He sounded rather pleased with himself

14

for having arrived at so much information about a personal aspect of Andrew's life.

"Her parents are in Georgia," he said. "Visiting a cousin. A second cousin. For as long as her father's having a gay time and there's a shilling in his pocket, I understand. He's supposed to be investigating the Colour situation. Some people don't deserve to have children."

Andrew didn't talk much about his domestic affairs, anyway to me, but I knew he had a sister who had managed to marry a journalist with not much time for family commitments. Their daughter had been at a boarding-school somewhere. It had been Andrew who paid the fees. This was something it had amused him to tell.

"She left last term, you know. I gather she got here by telling Andrew he was the only member of the family she could bear to live with. She was to have gone into something nice and secretarial, but now she's written a book."

Ammersgate didn't say this exactly with disapproval, but as if he foresaw it was likely to be unsettling for a girl rather than satisfactory. He added that the book was to be published soon, and that he supposed it was clever at nineteen to write anything.

I remarked that Andrew hadn't mentioned any of this to me.

"Andrew most of the time has a mind below such things; which I dare say is just as well for business. He'll tell you if it's a best-seller. I wonder he didn't mention it though, all the same—considering who it is. He should have married again, and had children of his own." Ammersgate removed a speck of something or

15

other from his trouser leg, looking knowing. "You must get Diana to tell you about it when she and Gerry do appear."

However, they didn't appear. That evening we didn't see any more of them.

Andrew came back into the room to say that any drinks they wanted now they'd have to have by themselves.

I found myself wondering a little as we went into dinner what Gerry was like. He was Sir Arthur Paley's son. I had heard the name, and Andrew placed it for me. " Plastics."

" Isn't their factory in Lincoln ? "

" So I'm told. The chap always seems to be here. Except when he's supposed to be. Much more of it and I'll send in a bill."

" Perhaps it's serious."

" With Diana ? "

" I tell her we shall have an old maid on our hands, the way she plays about," Ammersgate commented.

I said I shouldn't think that was likely.

Andrew then concluded his observations on the subject by remarking that Paley was a young fool of a boy who had been born with too big a plastic spoon in his mouth, and that he'd no idea why Diana wasted her time on him. " The only thing to be said for the chap is that he drinks lemonade. If that *is* something to be said for someone."

It was as we were finishing our fruit that Martin telephoned. I returned to the dining-room to hear Andrew saying then, "I think I will. Something of the sort. A girl needs a bit of family backing up, for God's sake."

16

What it was that he thought he would do I had no idea. But I was fairly sure he would do it.

He turned to me and asked about Martin, and I said the gloves had been a Christmas present from a girl-friend ; and after that—his fat, astute face looking all at once more satisfied—he began to talk about the bank rate.

The bank rate was important to us as a building society.

" It isn't as though any adjustment now would be enough," he said. " If general money rates take another twist. We'd better wait. The one bite at sour fruit."

That was his theme. He developed it until Ammersgate changed the subject to talk with renewed gossipy inflexions first of his sister's engagement, and afterwards of his mother's flowering shrubs.

I began to think about Diana. I wondered why she hadn't come back for the drinks, though Andrew had said you couldn't rely on her. And that night at home I thought about her.

I suppose that's the way it starts.

3

Andrew had suggested a board meeting for a quarter to eleven the next day. I was at the office early. When I arrived one of the typists, a girl named Betty Shaw, was sitting on the edge of her desk, eating a sandwich. She looked up as I came in, and got off the desk.

"It isn't tomato," she said, with the beginnings of a smile.

"Well, that's something, I suppose."

At once she became reminiscent and conversational. "Do you remember what a sight I looked? I never want to look like that again!"

The last time her eating of sandwiches in the office had concerned me was when they had given her tomato poisoning.

Though I dare say tomato poisoning is a slightly comic-sounding complaint, I hadn't found it amusing at the time. Moreover, one thing had led to another. For me. I could remember the whole episode very well: though I didn't want to.

"Especially this week," Betty was continuing. "Tom's coming on leave."

"Then have a nice time."

I went on into my own room.

My room was at the top of two or three polished stairs leading out of the typists' office. I liked it very much. The furniture was cedar, and looked warm against the paler wood of the floor, and the walls, which had been panelled. It had double windows to let in London or shut it out at will. There was a reproduction of Manet's ' *Villa at Rueil* ' which I had thought beautiful, its colours beautiful, and at any rate more or less appropriate to a building society.

I loved my room, and I loved the work I did in it. It was my father who had started the building society.

When I had closed the door I heard Miss Bowyer open hers.

18

Miss Bowyer had been engaged by him thirty years ago. She said, " Miss Shaw, how many times must I ask you to restrict your eating to the proper place and time ? What do you suppose Mrs. Allart thought ? "

However, what I thought as I turned to the mortgage applications on my desk, what passed through my mind, was : I wonder if it's voluntary, getting like Miss Bowyer. I wonder if it's something you can consciously not do. Over thirty years. With a vital part of you utterly deprived.

One of the applications was from somebody called Isaiah Jepson.

The board meeting began ordinarily. Andrew talked first, his back as usual to the high windows of the board-room, his heavy, determined-looking head thrown into relief, and we, the rest of us, listened in our usual places round the table : Julian Floyd, the accountant ; Lord Valrose, whose name was an asset and whose presence —he had taken Ammersgate's place—was more profitable than might have been imagined ; Rivers ; Lawrence ; Ellis, the secretary, slightly built, efficient, a smoother of ways. Brilliant rectangles of blotting paper stared blankly up at us.

The business of the meeting was discussed.

The blotting paper became less blank.

Then tea and cakes were brought as usual by the caretaker.

It was when we had finished that Andrew made his reference to Mr. Jepson. He had been glancing through the pile of forms in front of him ; now he said, " Isaiah. Chap's a Scotsman, I suppose."

"A coloured gentleman," Ellis said. "A West Indian."

"A few more of them and we'll have our own tribe."

It took only that, just that—and when it happened it rather endeared him to me—for Julian to say, his normal friendly expression changing a little, " The colour of the borrowers surely isn't very relevant." It wasn't that his expression became less friendly, but that it became more immediately engaged.

Andrew reached for a share certificate lying on the table, and signed it. " My dear chap, don't go putting me up for the Ku-Klux-Klan. It's the colour of their money I'm interested in, not their skins. We want to watch it, that's all. You wouldn't deny they can be pretty feckless. It's in the blood. They aren't cut *out* for home ownership."

" Mr. Jepson isn't ' they', of course."

" He's as likely to be unstable as the rest of them."

" I'm afraid, whatever people are, if you attempt to deny them necessities you only make them worse than they have to be." Martin had said love was a necessity. Now this was what Julian said ; they were his exact words. And afterwards I was to use them against him, as if it was a matter of life and death.

However, such reflections were of no great interest to Andrew. He began to look bored. " Granted, granted," he said ; " but you don't grow fat on foreclosures "—and to end the discussion he turned to me. " Didn't flatten anyone going home last night then, Judith ? "

I smiled at him. " No."

"Good." He looked round the table. "Well, I suppose we'd better be getting on."

"Oh, Andrew, by the way—Diana was all right, was she?"

"That reminds me. Yes, she was all right. Except that the girl's got no idea." His manner, suddenly, was more personal. "Turned up about two. Some tomfoolery with that boy. I didn't get to the bottom of it. You can see the sort of home-life she's had, though. Parents all over the place, and her staying with God-knows-who, up to God-knows-what. Absolutely no idea." He made a sound to express his feelings. "Anyway, I was going to talk to you about her. Hadn't she better have a party? Pre-publication cocktails. Something of that sort. Cushion her a bit against the financial dottiness of *writing* a book." I would never have thought of Andrew's face as fatherly ; but that, almost, was what it looked for a moment now. "We've got to sell a couple of copies somehow," he said. "I don't want my niece down the drain. Well, what do you think of the idea?"

"I should think it would be very helpful."

"I'll see what I can do. I'll begin now. Can you come?" He picked up a second share certificate and glanced at it. "Another Reverend. Diana wants you to. I should hope she wants to explain to you about last night."

4

I went to the party with Julian Floyd. Soon after Martin
and I had been divorced, he had asked me if I would
marry him. I think he thought it would be mutually
advantageous. Certainly the advantages to me must
have seemed rather obvious. As for him, while he had
never shown any sign of being ambitious to a disagreeable
degree, it was clear that he saw his life as a matter for
carefully considered action ; perhaps that was how he
saw everyone's life. And, so far as my job was concerned, anyway, I might reasonably have been considered
a 'good match' for him. Probably he was surprised
when I refused his offer of marriage. He suggested,
diplomatically, that I had lost confidence through making
an initial wrong choice, and added that he would try to
persuade me to change my mind. In the meantime, was
his friendship any use to me?

"Julian, I shan't change my mind."

But I was very glad of his friendship.

He was forty. As an escort he might have been des-
cribed as ' desirable '. He was still extremely handsome ;
and very big, comfortably over six feet tall. If I could
think of a word to convey the exact opposite of ' callow ',
that is the word I would use to describe him. He had
lightish hair which he kept neither long nor short, and
nice hands. He read Trollope and detective stories, and
played good tennis ; and knew everything about account-
ancy. His clothes were mostly rather formal ; and his
manners gave the impression not that he expected people

to please him but that he wanted to please them. I don't think I ever knew anyone less boorish.

He was obviously unusually *sympathetic* in his attitude towards people. Whether this was that he just naturally liked them, or that he consciously imposed on himself a Christian duty of charity, I didn't know. He didn't talk about himself in connection with things of that sort. However, I knew he was one of the few youngish people of my acquaintance who went regularly to church on Sundays. Occasionally—her attendances were conventional rather than religious—he went to a service with the aunt who had brought me up. Such conventional attendances might not have been altogether out of character in his case ; but all the same I rather assumed he was seriously religious. For one thing I had heard, though I wasn't certain it was true, that he had been confirmed when he was already adult.

He called at my flat to take me to the party. He said, " It wasn't kind of you not to have lunch with me."

" I was at the hairdresser's until after one."

" I had a very dull lunch." He kissed my cheek. " But at least you weren't wasting your time. You really do look very nice. Ivory makes you look beautifully remote."

It was like him to call my dress 'ivory' ; he would never have called it ' off-white '. His compliments were a pleasant routine. " The ear-rings are perfect."

" Martin gave them to me. A long time ago."

" In that case, should one wear ear-rings from an ex-husband ? May I give you a much nicer pair ? "

" Julian, we must go. The party will be over."

23

We had meant to be late, but not as late as we were. The traffic was impossible even by taxi-drivers' standards, and we arrived at Channing House when drinks were already being refused. The board-room was crowded. You couldn't see the people for the party. We stood in the doorway trying to discover people we knew.

"Andrew has done well," Julian said softly. "At a glance : Fleet Street, and the power behind a brewery. I was at school with that fellow." He had been to a famous school. He was proud of his school, and it had left its mark on him without keeping him a schoolboy at heart. "Arthur Paley's son's here, too. Look, by the window."

I looked, and saw Diana.

She was standing next to Gerald Paley, her hands in the pockets of her skirt. On one pocket, in big, white, interlinked script, was D.Q. : Diana Quendon.

I felt as if I was seeing someone I knew quite intimately but hadn't seen for a long time.

She was darker than I had remembered. She reminded me, I found, of Italians, Greeks, the Mediterranean ; not so much her features, which suggested it only very slightly, just enough to raise the possibility, but her colouring, the type of skin, the faintly mauvish pink mouth becoming visible through her lipstick. Her hair, now—its line broken, spikily, appealingly, at the back of her neck on her blouse's high nylon collar—looked almost black. Her blouse was white, her skirt a rather uncompromising blue.

Each detail of her appearance, each unimportant detail, was of immense interest to me.

24

Watching her in the moment before Andrew exclaimed Julian's name, and mine, I found myself absorbed.

Andrew took us over to where she stood.

She was saying, " Only it isn't the kind of book that *has* cocktail parties, or even lemonade and buns." When she saw us, she exclaimed, putting pleasure in her voice, " Oh, Julian—hallo. Mrs. Allart."

At this we all said suitable things until Andrew remarked that he hoped it *was* ; the kind of book.

" Oh, Andrew, why ? " She turned to him, saying it with charm. " I'm beginning to think that with your backing it hardly matters about the book."

He was pleased. " All the same I can't work miracles."

" Well, you've got Mrs. Allart here. I was quite certain she'd decided not to come."

" On the contrary I came by taxi, to be sure of coming."

She laughed. " You might have left your hand-brake on ? " Then she said, " I'm sorry about what happened ; for not coming back. We had a kind of——" Briefly she looked at Gerry. " Accident. You must have thought me very rude, but I didn't mean to be. I was going to come and say hallo."

Gerry was in his early twenties, I never knew exactly how old ; he was tall, and what is called ' wiry ', with an alive face, and a crew-cut. Everything about him suggested energy and vigour and expectation. Even his thick, dry, coppery hair looked as if sparks could be struck off it. Diana seemed to like him, or at any rate to have some sort of quite intimate relationship with him. He called Andrew ' sir '. There was no doubt that Andrew didn't like him.

25

I didn't think about it at the party. One doesn't as a rule think much, anyway, at parties. But I thought afterwards about something Ammersgate had said : that Andrew should have had a daughter of his own ; and I wondered if in essence that's what his antagonism was, the antagonism of a father towards the young man, any young man, who could never be good enough for his daughter. And then I wondered how I would have felt about my children ; if I had had children. But I wasn't going to have children.

Meanwhile, Andrew took my arm.

" Another drink," he said.

As we stood with our drinks he told me about some firm I should put my money in, always generous with his market acumen. " It's a case of looking sharp, though," he said.

He was still discussing investments when Julian came up to us to say that someone was looking for him ; I think it was Mrs. Rivers. She was very fond of Andrew.

He went off through the crowd.

I saw him have a word with Ammersgate, who was re-arranging things on a tray. Momentarily the mild, high-pitched voice rose above the declining party. " My mother abominates ash in saucers."

Julian glanced at his watch, and said to me, " Half past. Would you like some dinner ? "

" If you aren't doing anything else."

" Another drink, and an olive or two, and we'll go."

" I've really had enough. I'll just see if my seams are straight, and——"

" You have survived the party very well."

26

" Elizabeth Arden against the rest. All the same I'll just make sure. Then we must say something nice to Diana."

" She's at present in conference with television."

The man I had been told came from television was talking to her about cricket. He and Gerry had once played in the same team together. She looked up as I passed them—and I found myself talking to someone I knew who ran a travel agency. At the door, I heard her say, " Oh, well, *Gerry*.—But what would you expect, if it was Gerry ? The elder sons of industry are a cut above human."

" That's just where you're wrong." He laughed, looking straight at her, into her eyes. " The thing about me is, I'm *only* human. And if I chain up my Adam it makes him whine."

" How dreadful. You sound like fate," she said.

I went out of the room.

I had put on more lipstick and combed my hair when she came to the cloakroom. Ammersgate's sister had told me about her fiancé, and sent her love to Martin ' when you see him ', and gone, and I was alone. I was feeling round the back of a shoe, which had been hurting.

She said, " Julian said stockings, not shoes."

" Julian, as usual, was accurate. It was really seams. Suffering doesn't have to show." I put my shoe on properly again.

" I expect it's because he is an accountant."

" I expect so."

" They're very nice shoes."

" They're not very comfortable. They seemed nice in the shop."

" Heels as high as that are always a calculated risk." She paused, then went over to one of the basins and began washing her hands.

We both spoke at once.

" I've been meaning to say I hope your book will be a great success——"

" I've often heard Andrew talking about your father, and how he started the Channing. He practically *was* the Channing, wasn't he ? He must have been quite an unusual man."

" He began with about a hundred pounds. It was more or less his life, of course."

" And now it's more or less yours." The remark was half a statement, half a question, and she glanced round to smile at me as she made it. The smile was swift.

When I had made some sort of reply to this I said again I hoped her book would be a success, and asked her if she was going to write another one.

" It's what I'm supposed to be doing now, but I think I must be deranged. After all, as if it really mattered." I raised my eyebrows. " When writing a book isn't even nice. I certainly never meant to be a writer. I only meant to write a book. But it seems to be rather hard to stop. You know, I can't decide which is worst : before, during, or after. There's a man to-night told me the only thing to do with criticism is treat it as a sign of eccentricity in others. A man who reviews books."

" I expect he should know."

28

" Well, he might ; but *I* could *review* books."

" I'm sure you can write them. Diana, I must go."
It was curiously pleasurable, calling her Diana. " Julian
is waiting for me. I'm having dinner with him."

" Is it fun having dinner with accountants ? "

" I like having dinner with Julian."

We went back to the party together.

The last thing she said to me was, " I hope you like
my book."

So the next day I sent Betty Shaw out to get a copy.
The party, a success, was in the paper ; I wondered
very much what the book was like.

I'm not a book critic, and I'm not sure really what
one should look for or deplore in books, but I thought
as a writer she was good. I liked her because of her
intelligence, and because of her failure to be exclusively
intelligent ; because she wrote with a kind of intelligent
watchfulness, and with glints of wit, yet was as emotionally
receptive as any taste could have wished. She told the
story of some girls from a school in England going to
stay the summer in a French convent. Just that. But
the girls came whole-heartedly to life ; their Paris convent and the France they saw felt real—with smells, and
nostalgic scenes from the window, and noises, and things
to touch.

I thought she had an exceptional gift for taking one
right into her life of nineteen-year-old thought and
feeling ; of nineteen-year-old new experience.

She seemed to have set out to be hard and clear,
consciously unsentimental, detached, but she kept getting
thrown off this course by gusts of feeling : feelings of

love, for things and places, of excitement, or anger, or doubt.

Doubt, noticeably, had its place in her book. Mostly doubts about herself, and living. She was rather pre-occupied with ' living '.

She also had certain fond doubts about the French.

I looked through the pages again, remembering that somewhere she had written, 'The French have an amorous vivacity ; I don't know if they have tenderness —having neither.'

Then Martin telephoned.

The following day she sent me a copy of the book herself.

I wrote her a note saying I had enjoyed it. The note sounded conclusive, and vaguely discouraging ; I eventually tore it up.

That evening I telephoned a theatre agency about seats for a revue Helen, a friend of mine, had seen and said was good. I asked for Saturday. If she was busy, if she couldn't come, or didn't want to, that would be that.

5

We sat in a theatre half light from the brilliance of the stage. I was conscious of her next to me. She sat with her coat hung round her shoulders. It was velvet, and made her look indulged, slightly queen-like. The revue was the usual intimate, bright business of two pianos, and glancing innuendoes : jokes that were blue but didn't dig you in the ribs.

There was the recurrent joke about pantomimes, dressed up in something or other new. She smiled at it neither more nor less than at the other jokes. She appeared without innocence, and without any particular readiness to enjoy or be amused by references to sex. In profile her face was less pretty, more beautiful.

When we had first met earlier that evening she had seemed much shyer than when I had seen her last. She was very polite. In terms of friendliness we hadn't taken up where we had left off. She thanked me for asking her to come, and we talked almost formally about her book.

" I'm so glad you liked it."

" I liked it very much."

" Of course, it's only to amuse. It doesn't mean anything."

" I didn't think that."

She took care to be becomingly modest. She played down the good reception it had had, making me think rather of young, serious actresses being questioned on television about their new success. " Oh, well, but it takes a very remarkable book for anyone to *buy* it," she said.

It had already sold more than Andrew had expected.

" Do you feel now like getting on quickly with the next one ? "

" Oh, yes." She might or might not have meant it.

I found myself feeling as if confronted by this mood ; experienced something resembling disappointment because of it.

However, in the theatre and the imperfect dark she began to catch the mood of the revue, forgetting about her careful politeness and restraint. It happened quite obviously : the easy flow from one mood to another. At the beginning of the interval her conversation about the coffee and the items we had seen so far and the plays on the back of the programme had already been affected ; by the time we came back to our seats from the cloakroom it had all the light fluency of chatter.

She was telling me about a Belgian woman she had met on the train coming up from Westhaw. She told the story without malice but rather as if, after all, the best one could do with human relationships was make an entertainment of them. She grew animated with the telling of it. It didn't seem to occur to her that it might not perhaps be the ideal story for telling to me.

Apparently in fifty minutes the woman had introduced and related a detailed history of her marriage, which had just ended.

" So she said to her husband—*mais comme j'ai lutté, mademoiselle, pour le garder, mais, mon Dieu, comme j'ai lutté —' tu peux nous garder tous les deux* '. But the other woman said—*dure, vous savez, mademoiselle, mais dure : si jeune— ' tout ou rien. Vous avez eu votre tour, maintenant c'est le mien* '. And at last she said to herself, ' *Il sera plus digne de le laisser partir . . .* ' And there she sat less *digne* than anything I've ever seen. Honestly, Mrs. Allart. All ornaments and glitter. Women should be elegant. Don't you think they——? "

But she had become so intent on what she was saying

she had stopped looking where she was going, and didn't see the step leading up into the theatre.

She caught hold of me to save herself.

For an instant she was too surprised to say anything; then she said wryly, " Perhaps *you'd* better talk now."

It was as she was waiting for me to go into our row that she said, all at once perfectly natural and unthinking, in the tone one might use for a close friend, " Your programme's under the seat. Don't you want it ? "

I bent to pick the programme up. The lights faded; and she smiled at me.

The evening had come into its own; all the more enchantingly because of its first disappointment.

Outside the theatre afterwards we faced each other, undecided.

" A car in London's getting useless. I'm parked more or less in Soho Square."

" I can't remember where Soho Square is. It isn't terribly far from here—is it ? Couldn't we walk ? "

" What about your train ? Don't you want a drink, or—— ? "

" I've lots of trains," she said. " Anyway, till half-past eleven."

" That doesn't leave us a great deal of time."

" Till thirty-four minutes past eleven."

" We could catch the last one at Langley."

" Wouldn't you mind ? "

" I like driving at night. Especially out of London."

" So do I."

We walked through the little, food-smelling streets.

33

"Julian says he hasn't a car because he's unmechanical, but really it's because——"

"He's unmechanical?"

I laughed. How easily one laughs when one feels happy. "Yes, I know; but——"

"Anyway, I can't imagine he'd invent it as a cover for some unmentionable other reason. Can you?"

"—but it's really he's too clever to be bothered with one in London."

"I love cars," she said. "Anywhere. You're making too much fuss about London. You just have to be a bit ruthless, that's all. My father had the most marvellous car once. My mother was left some money. It was so long she kept forgetting the back. People were mostly rather sweet to her about it. She's that kind of person. But, anyway, they had to get rid of it when the money had gone. For one thing, it *quaffed* petrol."

Her expression hadn't changed when she mentioned her parents. But she went on quickly to something else. "If you hadn't asked me to come to-night," she said, "I was going to a boxing match."

Her heels sounded like chatter on the pavement. She had pulled her belt tight; too tight for her coat, but it emphasised with charm, almost voluptuously, that she was slim-waisted and tall.

"I didn't want you to put anything off."

"I would have done. But, anyway, it was only Gerry. Not that I don't like Gerry. He's lots of fun."

"Do you like boxing?"

"I've never seen it. I don't expect I'll mind. It's rather stupid, but they can always stop. It will be

34

interesting to see the people. I don't think I'd like bull-fighting much."

" Does Gerry want to take you to a bull-fight ? "

" No. I just thought of it. He saw one once, and didn't care for it. I think he thought it was a bit unEnglish."

" *That's* on the face of it indisputable."

" He has his conventional side."

" If it's conventional not to like bull-fights, I am."

" Aren't you, anyway ? "

" Oh, now, what do you want me to say to that ? The answer is—probably ; by inclination."

She smiled.

Now, as we walked, I had a feeling of personal association with her. It was as if we had become a small independent world in the streets, she and I—passed by people who were strangers to us, but no longer strangers to each other. We were the start of a human relationship.

Saying that love differs in origin from friendship is saying what is obvious. The difference, I suppose, is the tension, insubstantial and elating, which goes with even the possibility of physical pleasure. I touched her fingers as we walked ; lightly, ambiguously. Her fingers for a moment, in a friendly way, closed on mine.

The feel of her hand, a girl's hand, soft, delicately veined, the nails long and varnished, released in me a sudden gentleness towards her.

" You know that evening when Gerry and I didn't come back ? " she said, not pausing in her conversation. " Do you know what really happened ? "

35

I asked her what had.

"He *wouldn't*. He kept on driving—for miles. It started because I'd been out with someone else. We were terribly late meeting our friends. He wanted to make me say I loved him. He does do crazy things like that. He simply wouldn't stop."

"And his price for stopping was too high?" I had wondered, though it was apparently without importance, who her friends had been; who she had been out with.

"Well, I don't love him," she said. "Not his way, in the least."

"What is his way?"

She laughed. "Gerry's rather susceptible to sex." Then she went on, "Rather susceptible to life, in fact. Much more than I am. It's one of the reasons I like being with him. He almost does for both of us. After all, even if you've missed the point, it's obvious, isn't it, life's got to be *lived*? It's so obvious, it's a cliché; and probably there isn't any other point."

"I should have thought you were living it very fully."

She looked at me. "Oh, you mean the book?" she said, as if she couldn't imagine what else I might mean. "Do you think books really have much to do with living? I think they can be just instead of it. And the tyranny. If Gerry guessed a tenth of the *tyranny* writing is, he'd simply give me up for mad; how, if you do it at all, you've got to do it with the whole of you. He puts not his faith in the pen, bless him. Or in the sword, for that matter. In a way, he is rather marvellous. Do you like Gerry?"

"Yes. Yes, I like him. What I've seen of him."

"Andrew doesn't like him much. Andrew thinks I'm mad. I think he thinks he might 'lead me astray'."

"Oh, well——"

She waited politely, but there wasn't anything special I was going to say.

She took over the conversation again. "Do you know, I'm finding out Andrew's really quite fond of me. I'd never have thought it, and it seems an odd thing to say about Andrew, but he almost fusses. Strangely enough, I don't hate it, though. It's even quite sweet. *He* asked me last night if I loved Gerry." She paused to glance at a child, a little boy, up late and playing outside one of the cafés. "But I don't love anybody. I haven't the gift of—oh, what? I haven't the gift of desire. Tough character. No heart, either. It's sad, isn't it?" Then she asked, in a different voice, "Do you think it *matters*—if it's love happens to be your blind spot? I mean, vitally. Do you think you can have any sort of life without it? Or be any sort of a person?"

"I think it's rather soon to worry."

"Oh, but one's nature doesn't change, you see. I'd like to be able to think I'll feel one day about someone the way my mother does about my father, for instance; but if I'm honest I don't think I ever will. I suspect I'm cold. I can't think why that should worry you, though," she added suddenly. "I'm only talking about myself because you're not talking about yourself. I'd really much rather you did."

I loved it that she should talk to me about herself. That she should talk so much, easily and confidingly,

37

amused and delighted me. I didn't take too seriously everything that she said.

We reached Soho Square.

She liked the Healey. She patted its bonnet. "But don't kill us," she said, "will you?"

"Martin said something like that. The first day I had it."

"It would be sad, now."

I noticed the 'now', without being sure whether it meant anything.

When we drove past Langley Green, she turned and looked at me.

"Mrs. Allart, no. It's too far."

"I won't insist upon being told that you love me."

"I suppose not. But you'll have so far to get home again."

"When I get home I shall only put on the radio and look for some dance music."

"Then I wish I were coming with you."

When one is made to feel charming, especially if one wants to be thought so, there is a kind of exhilaration in it.

I would have liked to put my arm round her—simply as a response, an end in itself.

She seemed to settle more cosily into the car. It felt a physical move towards me; I'm not sure that it was.

We had almost reached Westhaw before she asked me about Martin.

"When you said Martin—he's your husband, isn't he?"

38

" Yes."

She paused. " I suppose you must have been young when you were married."

" Not—desperately."

" Only Paul Ammersgate said you'd been married two or three years before——"

" Which makes me twenty-eight; doesn't it ? " I turned and smiled at her.

To my surprise, she blushed. " I didn't mean that."

It was nice—to be enjoyed—the blush ; not because it came from her embarrassment but because it was personal and warm.

" It wouldn't have mattered if you did. You could have asked."

" I don't expect I'd have liked to."

" You can ask what you want."

" Could I have asked why you don't live with him any more, and yet you're friends ? " Then she said, " No, I'm sorry. I'm being terribly rude."

" Not rude. But it's rather an involved story ; all about the tragic folly "—I put the words in inverted commas—" of ever imagining you can live your life as if you weren't you at all. I doubt if you'd want to be bothered with it."

Our lights shone on Andrew's gates, showing up ' Four Winds ' in the darkness.

I didn't go in.

" Good-night, Diana."

Suddenly she leant towards me. " You have been sweet," she said, " and you're a very good driver." And, as one woman may kiss another, she kissed me.

But what I felt, what my remembering senses felt, had nothing to do with what one woman may feel for another.

I turned the car round, and began driving, rather fast, back to London.

6

That Sunday Martin called at the flat. I was expecting him. His brother, who had been intending to return from Canada with his family, had now been offered a key job there and decided to stay, so that there were some arrangements with the Channing to be cancelled.

He sat in front of the fire, smoking a pipe I knew from years ago—as familiar as his Sunday casualness ; a casualness perhaps slightly more marked even, to the experienced eye, than that of his ordinary, everyday appearance. His brown skin, with its one or two deep lines, looked rather as though he had shaved for something the night before and hadn't shaved again. He could never shave satisfactorily overnight, as some men can.

When we had dealt with the business aspect of his visit he stayed on, talking of this and that.

I liked his presence in the flat.

" Where's your cornfield, by the way ? " he eventually asked.

My cornfield had hung over the fireplace. " It didn't go with the wallpaper."

" The wallpaper is very nice."

40

"It was Julian suggested it. And the curtains. I imagine probably he has an interest now in dry cleaning."

"I imagine probably his interest is still where it was. Do you think you'll marry him in the end?"

"I know that I shan't."

"Anyway, it's quite something making a bachelor *that* determined change his mind."

"He might have got tired of being a bachelor."

"Yes."

I didn't know really why Julian hadn't married before. The possibility had occurred to me that he didn't experience with regard to women feelings in the nature of an urgent force; though he obviously liked them, and was liked by them. His love-making so far as I was concerned had been light; lightly charming. But then, it had never got very far.

Martin said, "Well, it all looks extremely attractive. This enthusiasm for interior decoration is rather new, isn't it? I don't remember it from Gerrard Court."

Gerrard Court was where we had lived together—and where he was still living.

"I had less time then for inessentials."

"I'm still sorry about the Nash, though. There's a *Paul* Nash exhibition on Sunday. I've forgotten where. I saw it mentioned in one of the papers. I suppose you wouldn't——?"

"Helen's staying at the flat again this week-end. She's rather bored with school. My aunt has asked us there for Sunday."

"Well, you won't come to much harm with Helen and your aunt." He stood up. He looked solid, and

41

his age—both somehow suiting him. " Do you know it's half-past eleven ? I suppose in the circumstances I'd better take my departure and not advantage. I haven't a key to your flat any more. Which is more than you can say about mine."

" Martin, so I have. I hadn't given it a thought."

" Don't," he said. " Keep it in your bag. You never know in this life when things are going to come in useful."

7

" Helen, do you remember Miss Dennis ? "

Helen Becker let the curtains fall back into place. " I was looking at the lights," she said. " It's my peasant mentality." She taught at a girls' school just outside Aylesbury. Usually in the holidays she stayed a few days at my flat, and sometimes for week-ends. " I'm sorry. What did you say ? Yes, of course I do. My memory isn't going. Yet. Shy, cerebral person. She took Latin. Never looked as if she had much money."

She hadn't had much money. She had been up to her eyes in a large and motherless family that had somehow managed to send her to college.

" You liked her, didn't you ? Why ? "

" Why did I like her ? "

" Why are we talking about her at all ? "

Helen lit a cigarette, and sat down again in an armchair. She was drinking whisky. She drank a good deal now by anyone's standards. She had a horror of herself and her situation as she saw them. She saw herself as an unmarried school-mistress without sex-appeal getting older all the time.

She had said once, 'People who aren't married just go on growing more and more like themselves. Can't you see me at it?'

Another time, after rather a lot to drink, she had said, 'If I knew how to go fairly decently about it, the first thing I'd do is get myself robbed of my virginity.'

Now she said, "I practically never think about when we were at school. And never about Miss Dennis. She wasn't there five minutes, was she?"

"A term. She left because of me." It was said now. After the urge to discover Helen's reaction, after the indecision, it was said. I was conscious of my quickening heart-beat.

"Because of you?" Helen displayed her hands to convey that she had no idea what I was talking about. "Why because of you?" Her cigarette bounced a little between her lips, and she took it out of her mouth and held it, the smoke running up through her fingers. "What do you mean?"

Then, for the first time, over all the thirteen years, I attempted an explanation; tried to explain to another person something of what the situation had been.

When I had finished she said, "Good God," blankly.

She added, at length, "I'd never have thought she was that sort. She didn't look it. I mean, she didn't have a stride or an eton crop or anything. What happened?"

What had happened was that she had come into our

class-room at the beginning of one Christmas term ; and
I had liked her voice, and her hands, and the suit she
was wearing, a dark suit, with a pale blue jumper. The
jumper, rather touchingly, was cotton. I had heard
from someone she had a First in Classics. I forgot
about this.

I waited for her to begin.

She hadn't any confidence as a teacher, but she
managed a thorniness of manner in emergencies which
saved her from humiliation.

I didn't imagine, despite my preoccupation with her,
that she was any more conscious of me than of the thirty
others in the class.

" When was the first time she seemed to be interested ? "

It hadn't been like that, not ' seemed to be interested ' ;
the words themselves made something different of it.
But I answered, " A week or two later she was outside
the school. I don't know if she had been waiting. She
just said, was I going into the town because she was and
we could go together."

" So you went together. What else did she say ? "

" Nothing much, at first. Then she said I had a
nice complexion."

" She didn't waste much time."

" She didn't mean it like that. It was only a remark.
She said she had told her sister when she had written.
Her sister was very interested in her complexion and
used all sorts of things for it."

" So what did you say ? "

" I was surprised." And pleased. I had decided,
after a prolonged, anxious adolescent analysis of the

44

situation, that I had nice legs. I hadn't thought about my complexion. In any case it is mostly very fair skins that are praised.

We began meeting quite often after that. For the first few times it just seemed to happen; then we knew that it would.

" But what did you do ? What did you talk about ? "

" Oh, nothing. Anything." It hadn't mattered. We had simply begun wanting to be together. She had talked to me about all sorts of things, haphazardly and without talking down. Sometimes I didn't understand her, but it hadn't mattered.

Except once, when she had said, 'If they find my handkerchief floating on the river, don't tell them why.' But then she had laughed, her abrupt, soft laugh, and refused to explain.

The river ran right through the town. We stood looking at it, and I hadn't understood in the least what she meant. Only about the suicide's handkerchief. It's such recollections that remind me of being fifteen.

One Friday she gave me a letter. She handed it to me in the corridor, saying, ' Don't open it till you get home.'

I could think of nothing else all day. I kept asking myself why she had given it to me ; whether she was going to leave ; whether I would see her any more ; what she had to write, and couldn't say to me.

But when I read the letter it was only about books, and a play she had heard on the radio, and about herself : just ordinary things about herself, nothing that seemed to me at all urgent. It was very long, as if she had been talking to me for hours. She wrote, ' I wish

45

you were with me. I'll write to you instead.' I was relieved, and puzzled, and very flattered.

Incident by incident, emotion by emotion—remembered, then selected or rejected for recounting to Helen —the whole affair re-created itself in my mind.

My aunt had found me reading the letter, which wasn't surprising since I read it so often. She asked me who it was from, and I told her. I hadn't the experience yet for suspecting a need to be discreet. When she asked to see the letter I could hardly refuse.

She wasn't pleased.

" Well—when did things begin to happen ? " Helen mutilated the end of her cigarette on an ash-tray. Again the words weren't right, but again I let it go ; I couldn't have said quite why they weren't.

" I used to stay behind with her sometimes after school. We just stayed talking together in one of the class-rooms. Only one afternoon, then, she put her arm round my shoulders."

I suppose it needn't have meant very much ; or anything—but, to me, it did.

She was showing me a book her sister had sent her. It was second-hand. Walter de la Mare. I can't remember the title. There were puffing cherubs on the jacket. We had been talking about the jacket. She and her sister were fond of each other, though they weren't at all alike. Her eldest brother was in the army. She'd scarcely said anything about him, although she often talked about the younger ones, except that he had ' no self-respect '. I didn't know what this was intended to mean, and hadn't liked to ask her.

46

I had been glad when she had put her arm round me. I had wanted some such gesture from her.

It wasn't long before the other teachers began to notice something, anyway, of what was happening. And then we took to meeting away from the school.

We went to the pictures late one Saturday afternoon, and after we had sat a long time in the darkness she took hold of one of my hands. It was my first experience of physical excitement from contact with another person. I wanted the film to go on for ever. I had come to a hot country with an interior of mystery ; but without knowing whereabouts I was.

When the film was over we drank cups of coffee in the cinema restaurant. The suddenness of the chandeliers and the brilliant glass panels had overcome me, and rather than look at her I looked at our reflection against my elbow. I said, hardly knowing what I was saying, " My collar is grubby."

" It isn't a thing I should say to you—but I don't care about your collar. Judith——"

I looked at her then : and my shyness dissolved in the new sweet excitement.

Going home, in the empty darkness of a side-street, which was all we had, we kissed. I wasn't shocked by this, and it didn't seem to me that I had been seduced. My response to her, though it was timid, was undisturbed by any thoughts of perversion or sinning. I suppose I was too ignorant to have named accurately the nature of our relationship. Anyway, I loved her. For the first time I was in love.

If I understood that such a love must now remain

hidden, it was obscurely, intuitively, and not with a real understanding of why.

Love made equals of us. Safe in our intimacy I began to call her by her Christian name ; to argue with her if I wanted to ; to laugh at her if I wanted to. To gain confidence in my enjoyment of her.

Her patience and gentleness with me became invariable and, to me, passionately moving. That I should have been chosen for something so precious as her tenderness was at the very core of her magic.

But only because she was what she was, because her hands felt as they did, because of her unprotected look, the line of her throat and collar bone, because her flesh, the little flesh our innocent loving permitted, entranced and comforted me.

I didn't know *why* I should want to be comforted, the desire was diffuse and vague ; anyway, it was of no consequence.

At school we did what we could to conceal our feelings —and at home now I never mentioned her ; but it was an adolescent's passion I had to keep out of sight.

I've never been sure what my aunt guessed about Jean Dennis. I don't know what she found out. Her surface complaint to me in the end was that she wasn't 'keeping her place as a teacher should '. But the complaint involved questions and half-questions, embarrassment, an expression of mixed urgency and revulsion, above all a driving sense of responsibility, that brought us to the brink, I suddenly knew, of something unspeakable for her ; like torture or drug addiction, yet in some dark, imprecise sexual way more unfathomably deplorable than either.

I think it must have taken a kind of courage when she telephoned the school.

I don't know what she said.

What was said to Jean was that in no circumstances should teachers risk charges of favouritism.

There was no question of her being told to leave. It was simply suggested that she would be happier making a wiser start elsewhere. But being what she was, she might just as well have been thrown out.

The days we had left were sharp with time. I could scarcely be forbidden to see her. She taught me Latin. My aunt's opposition, now that she had done what she had, was coldly disapproving more than dictatorial, made no direct assault on my pride ; but my love, anyway, threatened now and impeached, engaging a passionate loyalty, had burned up beyond the reach of dictation. On the last day of that term, when she went back to Carlisle, to-morrow was worthless to me.

My father gave me a pound, struck by my wretchedness.

She wrote to me, at a friend's address. She said she would come to London again when she could. She signed her letters ' All my love, Jean' ; but her letters didn't resemble what our relationship had been. Perhaps she was old enough to recognise defeat.

Mine were more ardent.

Yet I was the one to end the affair. And I ended it finally because, without her, and without any adult understanding of what wasn't normal, I began to succumb to the moral atmosphere I was breathing and to desire

49

normality, other people's normality, which now put me apart from them ; the normality of kissing a boy and talking about it afterwards. My sense of sin, delayed —artificial and impermanent—became all the same overwhelming.

Later, when there had been boy-friends to kiss, in an attempt to be like everyone else, my indifference to them had never faltered.

Adolescence had passed : I had abandoned the attempt.

What I was taught then was that the good homosexual is promiscuous and gay. What I learnt was that I was neither particularly promiscuous nor gay.

I met Martin at a time when, though the character of what I sought had changed, I was ready for letting myself believe that liking him so much was near enough to loving him, would turn to loving him ; and that I needn't, after all, solve the insoluble outside the main sexual pattern.

I had become a year or two older than in the weeks after Jean Dennis had gone, when my conscience had unwillingly maligned in her absence what had been lovely and natural in her arms ; when I had begun to desire the fresh start—with my emotions untainted and ordinary.

That was when I told her I had fallen in love with a boy.

I had two more letters from her. I didn't dare to open either of them. I knew at heart with what joy and ease I could fly back into what I saw as sin.

She didn't write any more.

50

I took all her letters to the bottom of the garden and burnt them there. It was intended as a final, cleansing break. It left me disgusted with myself.

Afterwards I had cried.

Helen frowned, and tapped an ambered nail against her teeth.

At last she said, " Well, I suppose I can make something of it on your side. Adolescent crush."

It was with some such idea I had deferred the truth myself.

" Rather drastic," she added. " I thought it was usually gym mistresses, anyway. But her! How on earth old was she ? "

" Twenty-four."

" Then what in heaven's name was she getting out of it ? " Her tone changed. " Of course one knows about queer women. There was some sort of fuss about a couple of girls at college. But I can't say I've ever come up against it. Have you ? I mean, since you were grown-up." She didn't wait for an answer. " No woman's ever kissed me under the mistletoe."

" Perhaps you wouldn't like it if she did."

" I'd conclude she was mad. As for the Dennis woman, if it had been one of the boys it wouldn't have been so crazy. Some of those sixth-form boys were practically men. Still, perhaps a boy wouldn't have wanted——"

" I don't think boys have anything to do with it. It's a question of wanting a girl. The things a girl is; in the same way as one might be attracted by men."

" You seem to know a great deal about it." Suddenly

51

she laughed. " If you carry on like this, you'll end up having me thankful for your nail varnish."

" I don't think nail varnish has anything to do with it either."

" Well, I don't know what has to do with it," Helen said ; " but I do know I don't think much of her morals. I suppose she couldn't help being whatever she was : psychology or glands or something, isn't it ? But she might have messed up your life. You were only a kid."

Younger than that I had cared about the heroines in films, not the heroes ; and worshipped a girl cousin, not a boy. Jean Dennis had been a part of my life— but perhaps she had been only an inevitable part.

I dare say it can be different.

Helen said, " My God, though, some women defeat me ! "

I didn't reply. I scarcely knew what to reply. I knew it was because of Diana I had been talking to her about Miss Dennis at all.

8

The Channing had its regular board meetings on the third Thursday of the month. ' To keep an eye on each other ', it amused Richard Rivers to say. He was an elderly, conscientious man with a lot of other interests, and prided himself, in common with a good many elderly men, on being busy.

On the Thursday after Helen had been for the week-end

again, we found ourselves with a disagreeable extra to be considered. Miss Bowyer had discovered Davis, the caretaker, stealing money from the typists.

It was a rather small sum that was involved and so far as we knew it was the first time anything of the sort had happened. Several of us were inclined to tell Davis to see it didn't happen again, and leave it at that. Nobody but Rivers wanted to take any legal action. However, Andrew was adamant about getting rid of him.

" This is a building society not a moral re-armament group," he said. " If the chap's a thief, he goes. It might be my money next."

I didn't particularly care to think of its being Andrew's money. Mostly because it was Andrew who had given him the job. Andrew didn't like to be made a fool of.

He was perfectly within his rights, of course. One could scarcely insist on keeping somebody who had been taking money, when it wasn't unanimously agreed. Andrew had his way, and it was decided Davis was to be sacked.

Julian, who had been against it, was still looking unhappy about the decision as he introduced the question of making new investments before the next publication of our accounts.

We talked over this question of the investments. Andrew was brilliant. There was a kind of virtuosity about his vivid deployment of facts and figures in argument. It always fascinated me ; on this occasion, too, I was glad to have my thoughts distracted from Davis.

53

However, the discussion for some reason seemed to go on and on, in the end for pleasure rather than business; it became a debate on their own affairs between Andrew and Rivers.

I began half listening, then hardly listening at all ; words, sentences, parts of sentences, began to be imposed more or less meaninglessly on my inattention.

'War Loan . . . Funding Loan . . . something under 82 . . . redeemable at par.'

Until suddenly, again, I was thinking of something else ; the something I had thought of repeatedly since my evening with Diana.

I was at a loss when Lord Valrose all at once asked me, " Do you agree with that, Mrs. Allart ? "

I looked at him.

" Do you agree with Mr. Jefferson that if the country goes to the dogs altogether, your equities will suffer as much as your Government stock ? "

The question, out of its context, seemed pointless. I didn't know what to answer, having no idea what lay behind it. However, I knew it would have a point. When Valrose emerged from behind closed eyes with an abrupt display of interest it was at times rather comic, but never pointless.

Andrew laughed. " Whatever Mrs. Allart was thinking about," he said, " she wasn't thinking about investments."

Tea was brought in.

As we drank it, he added, handing me biscuits, " Anything on your mind, Judith ? "

" No." I took one of the biscuits.

54

There was a pause.

I could hardly tell him what was on my mind ; still less why.

It was very theoretical, so far as I was concerned, thinking about love in connection with his niece. Apart from anything else, quite apart from my own attitude, I didn't even know if the possibility existed. To like another woman, to offer her warm friendship, is not, after all, the same as being prepared—or able—to cross the frontier of normality for her.

But it was what I had been thinking about.

" I wondered if we were going to hear about Miss Salmon. I never quite know : what with you and now our accountant." Andrew began eating a biscuit himself. He went on, " Doesn't anyone want to accommodate Miss Salmon ? She isn't black but she's not only a woman, she's a needlewoman. And she has nothing like the money for buying her semi-detached villa."

" I don't know about Miss Salmon. I haven't seen the new applications."

" Oh, well, so long as nothing's wrong."

I smiled at his irony, and we looked at each other an instant with understanding and without rancour.

" Only when you have her here—and I can see that *happening*—for God's sake don't let her near me ! The grey and the fragile aren't up my street." Then he put aside his cup. " Talking of the little woman round the corner, by the way, I'm clearing off now. I've been detailed to go with Diana to buy her a dress. It's apparently inadequate a man should buy his niece a present—which is certainly all I said I'd do. I'm to

55

take an interest in the colour." He stood up : short, heavy, expensively dressed. " The man's angle."

" How is Diana ? "

" Getting bags under the eyes."

" The book's doing wonderfully."

" Now all that's wanted is the next one. But that's *another* thing I can see happening : us waiting. If she does any work it's one matter she's discreet about. Still " —and he laughed, as if it amused, even pleased him rather than otherwise that his niece shouldn't be working too hard—" aren't you only a young lady once ? "

" Always."

" Oh, yes, of course. I should keep off the subject. It isn't something I'm an expert on. Good-bye, Judith. Don't let Miss Salmon give you ulcers."

When the meeting was over, I went to my room to get on with some work there which would eventually have included Miss Salmon—but before I got as far Diana had knocked on my door and come in.

She was with another girl.

They stood in front of the desk with an air of purpose and high spirits, as though they were going to celebrate something ; as though they had only a moment to spare.

I saw her with an absolute pleasure : saw again the dark hair and eyes, the smooth, pale, the almost olive skin of her face ; its intelligence, its delicate, triangular femininity.

Though I was to know her face so intimately, know so intimately its different expressions, I never once saw it negative and empty.

56

Now it seemed to be warm for me—and my pleasure at once was followed by the desire, a desire not unlike the sensation of thirst, to be myself involved in whatever it was she was going to do.

" Mrs. Allart," she said, " do you mind that we've come to see you ?   Are you very busy ?   This is——"
She told me who her friend was, but I didn't see her again and don't remember her name.   I remember she behaved with a kind of friendly ordinariness, as if she had already accepted me on Diana's recommendation.
" We've had a sudden idea."

I said I wasn't busy, and offered them tea, which they refused.

Then Diana said, " We're practically on our way to a party.   The man Gerry stays with in London, it's his birthday.   We're going to help with the food.   He's quite near, at Victoria, so it wouldn't be far.   Will you come ? "   She paused, smiling at me.   " Come, anyway. whether you can or not."

" It will be all right.   There'll be lots of men."   The girl she was with laughed.   " I hear we're getting scarcer —I hope."

I looked at Diana.   It was true there were shadows under her eyes, but she seemed very gay ;   and while lack of sleep may be ageing in its effect on those who aren't young, for the very young it seems somehow to intensify their quality of youth.   She returned my look without speaking, but as though there were something between us, an understanding.   She asked me with her look to come.

When I said I couldn't it was some sort of reflex

action, like putting out one's hand in the dark to ward off anything that might be there. I didn't think about it, it wasn't a decision; it was simply an action.

She was very polite. She said it had been silly, anyway, asking me at such short notice. She refused to appear disappointed. But she didn't look at her friend. I think she had been sure I would come.

I felt repentant; as if I had let her down.

We said good-bye.

After they had gone Miss Bowyer brought me some cheques to sign. I asked for Betty Shaw.

Betty came looking doubtful. It was getting on for half-past five.

" I'm terribly sorry. I'm afraid I've had visitors. Would you mind staying a bit late? "

She said at once, " But Tom's meeting me."

" Oh, Betty. I didn't know. It's the advertisements, you see. They must be in before the week-end. Would he wait? "

She hesitated.

" I'd send out for some sandwiches. We could have tea in here."

" Could Tom? "

" Of course."

" All right," she said then. She opened her shorthand book.

" What was the last thing we said? "

" '. . . putting one's money to work not only for a dividend but——' "

" Oh, God, Betty, cross it out! Though why is it so impossible to say anything of the sort? There are

58

more futile things than helping people get homes. Put——"

"He'll be outside by half-past," she said.

Tom was a sailor, gingery, with red wrists coming out from the sleeves of his jersey. Betty thought he was wonderful. She typed the advertisements rather badly because he was there. When they went out together he put his hand an instant on her waist, urging her to go first, and she looked up at him, quickly, eagerly, and smiled.

"Thanks for the sandwiches," he called back to me.

I watched them go.

"It's a good thing they weren't tomato," she said.

I didn't want to smile.

I was glad when they had gone. I sat looking at the papers on my desk but didn't do any more work.

Tomato poisoning had made her face red and swollen, and her pulse race. At the hospital they had kept her there for tests.

It was while I was waiting that I had met Margaret Carpenter.

I've put off this part of the story once, but I think it's relevant to the rest ; at any rate it underlined for me what my exact position was.

She was a doctor at the hospital, a lung specialist. Tall. Perhaps forty. Perhaps rather more. I remember her less as a person than as a personality. When I first saw her she was coming down from the X-ray room, white-coated, carrying X-ray plates. She was smoking a cigarette. She looked tough, but dreadfully tired ; her lipstick had almost gone, her eyes had the half-closed look of exhaustion. Her face, with its clear bone structure, seemed thinner than it was. One could have liked her simply for being so tired.

Noticing me she paused, and asked me if I wanted anything.

I explained.

" The girl won't die," she said.

When she sat down it was as if she would have sat down, thankfully, anywhere ; but she began to talk.

We talked about Betty first, and then about her work at the hospital. Though she answered my questions in the somewhat illusionless way of overworked professionals, she didn't seem to mind answering them.

Eventually she asked me to have dinner with her.

I knew why, really, from the beginning. Sexual interest can be conveyed ; or it can be just unmistakably there, an unmistakable passage of feeling.

Married to Martin, I had been rigidly faithful to him. And afterwards, neutral in my pessimism, had done nothing, looked for nothing ; simply waited. Now, though I knew I would never love her, was someone to end at least the wretched frustrations of the body, and my personal, private isolation—someone I couldn't harm but only give pleasure to. And I responded to her interest.

It was the Autumn of the year Martin and I were divorced.

" I have to take Betty home."

" Just time for me to think about the dinner."

" Then—thank you."

She lived in a block of flats almost into Chiswick. That evening she had dinner sent up from the restaurant.

She was completely 'hospital weary'.

"There's one thing about that place," she said ; "it sees too much of me."

"It's sometimes the same whatever one does."

"I have no imagination. I can't imagine other people's lives. I can't imagine working for a building society. Do you like it?"

Yes, I liked it. I liked it extremely. I liked the nature of it, and the feeling I had that it was as near a social service as anything basically commercial could get ; something in me even found a curious temperamental satisfaction in the final inelastic, salutary necessity of doing everything within two columns of figures which stood for staying in business. I liked the light business ritual ; the conventions of business, quite apart from the fact that in our case they had eventual human point.

I loved my office. As I have said.

It was much more than an office to me. It was the one place, the only place since I had been grown up, where for any length of time I was without a sense of being badly adjusted to my environment ; of running fundamentally counter to life as a whole.

Nor did I attempt to explain to her how, in addition, my father had involved me in feelings of responsibility for something of worth, even of public worth, which was his ; which he had created, and developed, and which he had now left me to care for. My father and I had never been close, he had begun and ended for me as a dedicated business man ; but he had seen to it we had finally had the Channing in common.

61

She and I had finished dinner.

She walked to the fireplace, lit herself a cigarette. She had no white coat now. She was wearing slacks. They suited her. " I've never been in much danger of dealing with building societies. I've never been in any danger of marrying."

She turned and looked at me through the smoke ; it was the start of hazarding honesty between us.

The situation wasn't new to her.

She took us without clumsiness through the conversation that told us about each other—and back to her original point.

" Some homosexual women seem to manage marrying and fitting in," she said. " More, I imagine, don't. It's largely temperament, I suppose ; and circumstances. I came into contact with a woman last summer who'd been married half a lifetime when she met some woman or other who really found out her weak spot. She left her husband. At fifty. I don't know about her future ; I know she thought of her past as lost. Not that she probably wasn't going to think of her future as lost, too. Rather sooner than later."

" And her husband ? "

" God knows. At least if you don't attempt to conform, you can see to it it's only your own funeral. Try to make homosexuals do it, or tempt them to, and you just spread the trouble. I wouldn't have anything to do with it. Yet I'd rather work with men. On the whole I like them better."

" Marriage doesn't *help*."

Merely in talk one's isolation begins to lessen.

62

" What does ?   Do we know a cure ?   We don't know
the cause.   Or causes.   We talk about hormones, for
instance, and what the infant thought of its mother and
father.   We talk a good deal."   She grimaced.   " I've
done more than talk.   I handed myself over to a psychiatrist.   It seemed the thing to do.   But I might as well
have saved my time.   I'm not saying, of course, they
don't sometimes have something to offer.   For the more
amenable cases."

I looked at her.

Psychiatry was something that had been often enough
in my own mind.   But never without a feeling of hopelessness ; never without a complete inability on my part even
to *wonder* if such treatment—whatever its nature, however
I co-operated—could be of any help to me.

I had begun by believing I could change *myself*, and
come through experience to where I felt nothing could ;
felt it deeply and statically.   It wasn't a question of
resisting the idea of psychiatrists ; certainly not intellectu-
ally.   It was a feeling of complete certainty that a
psychiatrist could do no good.

The feeling was like knowledge.   I think it must be
very common—so integral, so absolute a part of one
appear one's own sexual desires ; so unlike an emotional
disorder.   It was what had kept me from the consulting-
room.

Even so, at a strictly mental level it was inevitable it
should recurrently seem, as she had said, ' the thing to
do ', to go to a psychiatrist.   All I had consciously
resisted was distress and embarrassment and pain to no
purpose.

Only my feeling was like *knowing* it would be to no purpose.

And what she said that day had an immense effect on me. It was almost as if she had clinched the argument ; ended the conflict.

" Anyway," she added, " when all's said and done, it's the world's out of step—as we know. And there's the question of being cut psychiatrically about ; being made into something appearing quite synthetic to us. One's personality as one knows it is at least one's own. In fact, it's oneself."

I thought about the remark, without answering.

She went on, then, " Another thing we *don't* know, by the way : why feel as I did about *you*, especially ? Instinctive ? A case of being attracted in the right quarter ? One can be mistaken—but not so often."

It was with this that she came to what I now saw as the one real moral issue exclusive to homosexuals ; the thing mattering incomparably most.

" I'm afraid it isn't very generally held that homosexuals only attract each other."

" Then let's say being attracted where there's a fair chance of success."

" Do you think heterosexual people can be made homosexual ? "

" I think," she said at length, as if going along with my thoughts, " there are a majority who couldn't. It works very much in reverse, after all. Look at your own experience of marriage. I also think there are some who might change in their behaviour for a time, but would go back with relief to what was natural for them." She

64

lit another cigarette. " But it's the people with the more or less dormant homosexual tendencies who present you with your problem or choice or whatever you like to call it. Leave them to themselves and they might get by, go with the swim. Wake them up to what they are, as you'll probably want to, because of what you feel in them, and they'll make the choice they have to make—though it's doubtful in the end whether they'll thank you for it." Suddenly she smiled. " But all this is of no immediate concern to either of us. Is it? There's really no need for my textbook oratory."

Her smile made me wonder if her toughness was unintrinsic, like the leather patches at vulnerable points on a man's jacket.

I was glad of the smile.

Not long before we were married, Martin had said during a discussion with a student of his, "In a civilised society, there's no solution to sex. You can only rub along." *He* had said that, and he was a man who loved women.

With Margaret Carpenter, later I remembered what he had said.

But you can only ' rub ' along within the limits of your own nature. That's the complication. When we made love it wasn't that it was awful, or that I could believe any more there was some dark unimaginable awfulness implicit in it ; it was that it failed.

Nothing I felt for her really had anything to do with her personally. In a way it was like using a person as a thing ; intolerable in any situation.

Afterwards I wanted to go away from her, and not see her again. That was the measure of its failure.

65

Generalisations can be very irritating. All the same I think it probably is true that a majority of women, any women, find it hard to separate their bodies successfully from what, for convenience, they call their hearts. Perhaps a majority of men ; I don't know.

As for the heart, it won't be coerced. It goes its own, self-opinionated way, and was never much renowned for using discretion.

To the homosexual, its decisions are a chancy, terrifying business.

At home, the evening of Diana's visit to my office, there was a letter from Helen. It informed me in typical Helen tone that a girl on her staff was getting married. A June wedding, she said. She had been invited as ' a foil to the bride ' ; to refuse might look as if she weren't delighted. Could I stand a further week-end of her then ?

There was something *about* the date, I couldn't think what. I answered the letter, but didn't make a note of it.

It was as I was going to bed that the telephone went. Just for an instant I wondered if it might be Diana, and wanted it to be.

It was my aunt.

" What do you think of Julian ? " she said.

" Julian ? "

" His new car."

I hadn't known he had a new car.

" Then perhaps it is a secret. But he had it with him yesterday. He came near here to see a client, and called in for tea. He showed it to me. It was very splendid. He seemed quite pleased with himself."

66

" He's always said he didn't want a car."

" Well, it is apparent that he does now—since he has bought one."

She went on to talk about our arrangements for Easter, which was why she had telephoned.

Diana's phone call came after I had stopped half thinking it might.

She said, " Oh, Judith——" There was a pause. Then, " Do you mind ?   Should I call you Mrs. Allart ? "

I can't explain just why this should have been exciting ; but it was.

" No.   I don't mind."

" I'm phoning for Andrew."

" For Andrew ? "   I had, as usual, seen him that day.

" He wants you to come to dinner.   When can you come ? "   Again there was a pause, and she laughed, rather quickly.   " You have to have lots of notice for things, don't you ?   Please come.   If you tell me what you most like eating, I'll get Jean-Pierre to have it for us. He's a marvellous cook."

9

Julian told me he was considering taking his car on holiday, but I didn't think any more about it.

I had begun seeing Diana.   Not a lot, but sometimes. We went to one or two concerts—a Bach concert I remember in particular—and several foreign films.   We didn't at once achieve again the intimacy of our first evening. For reasons more mine than hers, I think, we always did something specific, were entertained in some specific way, and then parted. I loved being with her, loved her physical presence, but was avoiding so far as I could the necessity of having an attitude towards her ; of being something definite in relationship to her. It was slightly more possible without close conversational contact than with it.

If I suggested anything she always agreed. She didn't suggest things herself. She didn't seem to mind a great deal what we did.

However, finally—after we had been to the theatre on one occasion and it was late—she said she was hungry and wanted to go to some coffee-stall she had heard of off Leicester Square. It was my turn to agree: so I did.

We drove through a dozen or more little side-streets, streets half closed down for the night now, given over to an air of shoddy vice, and looked for her coffee-stall.

There was a potency I hadn't been prepared for in this resemblance to an earlier situation : the lateness and the darkness, her presence with me in the car. I began to be intensely, sharply aware of her.

She had changed ; not startlingly, but obviously. She now looked more unconventional, more ' Left Bank ' —if that is still a possible term for explaining what I mean. However much actual writing she was or wasn't doing, she was newly in touch with a world quite different from the backgrounds which had previously influenced her, and she had reacted visibly to it ; had visibly become less of a rich man's niece and more of a ' writer '.

One of her new friends was somebody called Vic who

68

had written three novels and a book on sailing. She had told me she and Gerry had been to his flat the night before, with some jazz records. He lived, apparently, with a Chinese girl.

She said now, as if she herself had responded to the situation, the tone she used once more entirely, overwhelmingly personal, "Judith, do you think *I* ought to sleep with Gerry?"

But the question was out of the blue; and its nature unpalatable to me.

I slowed down for a group of people standing in the street ahead. "I don't know. How would I know? Do you want to? I should think that's rather important."

"Oh, I want to do everything," she said. "I meant, do you think that I *ought* to. Since Gerry's in love with me, and I see him a lot, and he can't be expected to live like a monk. I don't want to be paltry."

"Shouldn't it be someone you love more than Gerry?"

"But I told you, I'm not the kind of person who falls in love." Then she added, "Still, it might turn out for the best, after all. Just think how hard-headed I can be when I marry. I've decided to marry at twenty-five : a very rich publisher, for preference. Andrew says it's ridiculous ; as if there were any. Not that he wouldn't prefer the idea to Gerry. He and Gerry, by the way, have practically had words. Over politics. Gerry's a Liberal. At least, it was supposed to be politics. It was really because we got back late, and he kept on staying. Andrew hadn't gone to bed."

"Why twenty-five, especially?"

"Well, it's got to be sometime ; hasn't it? And by

69

twenty-five there's something a bit bare about that fourth finger. Oh, look—my coffee-stall. Can you see ? My coffee-stall."

The coffee-stall idea was quite absurd. We couldn't stay there five minutes. So much so, it seemed to have a kind of continuity when, back in the car, our conversation was resumed.

" Heavens," she said, brushing crumbs off her knee. She was still eating her bready hamburger. " I thought the one with the heavyweight's face was coming right in."

" You shouldn't have encouraged him." I hadn't meant my tone to be cold, but I could hear that it was.

" I didn't. Well, if I did, he *was* rather marvellous ; all polo-necked and primitive and ready to rape us. I didn't know you got men like that outside France."

" Do you like men like that ? Perhaps that is the sort of man you should marry."

" I don't know that I like them. I liked him to like me. I'm afraid I thought it was rather fun. Exciting. Like an apache dance." She looked at me. " You aren't annoyed ? "

But what I was, apart from preferring more ordinary ways of ending an evening, I suppose was jealous ; though it wasn't something I could admit to her.

I shook my head.

" I know it all turned out a bit silly in the end ; but it didn't matter. Did it ? " Then she added persuasively, " They thought you were marvellous, too." It was almost funny, that she should so misunderstand the nature of my jealousy. " I could just imagine them

70

all dying to be the exception who got you home and untidied you up and made you approachable."

" That's nice."

All at once she laughed. " And that's how you looked. Oh, Judith, darling, honestly—a human pencil skirt. Isn't that what they called them ? I felt like the Duke of Wellington. I don't know if you frightened the enemy, but——"

" Are you frightened now ? "

" No. Not now."

" Do you think I'm unapproachable ? " I just stopped myself from looking at her.

" No." Her voice was softer.

There was something in the silence that followed which could have become emotion between us. I felt it ; and could think of nothing unemotional to say, though I tried.

It was she who broke the silence. She told me, abruptly, with no sort of introduction—just, I think, in order to say something—about the letter she had had asking her to be on a television programme.

The moment was over.

" Diana, that's wonderful. Why didn't you tell me at once ? "

" I was saving it up. I was enjoying the idea of how you would say, ' That's wonderful '. Though it isn't particularly. My mother will laugh."

" Is she so very unbusiness-like ? "

" No ; well, bless her, she isn't *business-like*. But, anyway, I have to say ' in a few words ' what I'm working on now. You *might* call it advance publicity ; Andrew does. Personally, I'm not sure there's any better way

71

of putting people off. You start : the story's about a man and a woman——"

" I'm not put off."

" Oh, but you're my friend. Or you were, until to-night. Poor Judith. I'm sorry. I should have known the coffee-stall would be a mistake." She went on, " It's a magazine programme. Anything from polymers to Polynesians. I don't suppose you'd know about polymers—but Gerry and I have our dipole moments. That's a joke. I imagine it isn't very new, but it's very occupational. Oh, Judith, what a shame you don't go out with a chemist, too. So that you could appreciate it."

" You'll have to lend me Gerry : for my education."

" I wouldn't trust Gerry an inch with you. Perhaps I shouldn't you with him. My mother thinks Gerry's fabulously attractive. My mother will laugh," she said again. " Sitting on a settee with a television pretty boy ! I shall use the fee to telephone her."

" She'll be sorry she couldn't see you."

" *I* shall be sorry. I am the one who is sorry, where my mother is concerned."

" Are you sorry you didn't go to Georgia ? " I was suddenly able, for the first time, to ask it.

" Oh." She pursed her lips. " Oh, I doubt if I'd much care for my own end of the bus. Besides, one prefers not being too much of a nuisance—and I don't deceive myself I was family planned."

Instead, after this, of going straight to a girl-friend of hers, a Pat who was putting her up for the night, we sat in a café we found nearer home and went on talking.

72

Neither of us spoke any more about her mother. She told me about her room at school; the white, bumpy counterpane; and the mistress who had turned off the lights—always leaving a smell of antiseptic soap in the darkness. " But there was the nice one, the one with red hair, who taught us, so help me, deportment and drama ! "

She had written her book about France mostly at school.

" There was nothing much else to do ; now there is too much else. I am cut out to write very tiny books at very immense intervals. A publisher's nightmare. You see, in the *end* I shall have to marry one." From across the table, her face in her hands, she regarded me, smiling. She looked tired but not sleepy.

I made some sort of answer.

But when one is approaching the edge of a physical passion for another person—however it may be touched off, by pity, by a sense of the unattainable, or in any other way, whatever other sympathies may be involved, even more unchanging sympathies—it is the voice that absorbs rather than what is said ; the faint frown in the smile ; the hands, and the hair. Martin wrote a poem, the only poem I had ever known him write, about ' almond blossom showering ' in the back garden of one's heart. It was rather like that.

She exclaimed, " Judith, talk ! Don't just be sweet to me. Or how will I ever get to know about you ? "

" What do you want to know ? "

" Everything."

I laughed. " That's characterization ; not life."

And I suppose it is true that in real life our knowledge

of people, even the people nearest to us, or of ourselves, isn't thick and worked-out. We simply know certain facts, see certain things ; sometimes relate one thing to another, or dismiss a possibility.

But that night, all the same, Diana and I had moved nearer in our relationship.

The next day, we met again.

And afterwards began seeing each other much more often, our next meeting assumed ; as in a love affair.

10

She didn't get tired of the car, and one Sunday, when we had been out in it, we called to see my aunt.

This aunt who had brought me up was my father's only sister. She lived in Harpenden.

She didn't enjoy life ; so much of what life is repelled her. As a child I was chilled by this and—caring for her —felt under the constant obligation of trying to make her enjoy it more. Later I saw the futility of such attempts —but the sense of having to try continued.

I thought she might like to see us. Diana would be someone new. As for me, I suppose I amounted, then, to what she lived for.

She gave us tea, and expressed an interest in our affairs. When she had inquired about Andrew and his mother, and about Diana's book, she told the history of her house, a narrow Georgian house my father had bought for her before he died. She thought up a remark or two about historical novels. She even recalled some trifles of local news to entertain us.

None of it conveyed much about herself. She had a natural restraint, a natural undemonstrativeness—besides an iron respect for the keeping up of social appearances—which made her refuse, where she could, to show anything she was feeling, whether it was depression, or boredom, or affection, or what it was. I should have thought one would have needed to know her quite intimately to suspect that she felt her sixty-odd years hadn't been worth it.

But Diana could be perceptive : and as we drove back to London she was very quiet, her whole mood coloured by the afternoon.

She didn't make any direct reference to our visit, but when we were nearly home she said, " It must be awful to get old and feel the whole thing, really, has been a flop. Though I dare say it's what's going to happen to me. I'm that kind of person."

" More than most people ? "

" Yes, even more than that."

It had begun raining.

" Is there anything you especially want to do ? Would you like to come back to the flat ? "

She hadn't been.

She looked at me. " Yes, please."

We left the car in the road outside, and went up to my flat.

But once there she sat about on the edge of things, refusing to settle.

" I'm going to have a white carpet. If ever I get married."

"I thought it was definitely to be to a publisher. I only have a white carpet because I have nothing better to do with my home."

"And curtains like yours."

"Then don't live in London."

"Oh, I shall live in London," she said—but she was wrong : about the carpet and the curtains, and about living in London when she was married.

She sat looking at the carpet.

"Why are you sad?"

"I'm not."

"Why are you looking like that?"

"A cheerful expression gives one lines."

"I think I would almost rather have the lines."

"It's all right for you ; when you have lines it will suit you."

"I meant, I don't like you to look sad."

"Don't you?" Then she said suddenly, "Judith, can I have a wash?"

I gave her a towel, and while she was gone put on the television.

She came back from the bathroom without make-up, the ends of her hair damp ; this, and her complete absence of manner now, a gay manner, a sophisticated manner, any manner at all, anything to cover up her mood of depression, created of themselves a new degree of intimacy between us.

She began to look at my books. "I wish I *didn't* think everything was futile and a bore," she said, picking up *Antique Dealer*.

"Perhaps if we watch the play you'll be less bored."

76

"I didn't mean that. I'm never bored with you. I bore other people talking about you. I can't think why you should be so important."

I was sitting on the settee. Instead of sitting there too, or in one of the armchairs, she came and sat on the floor in front of me. She sat straight, separate.

At length she said, "I wonder what sort of money they pay for a commercial script. How worthwhile it is. Or isn't. I'm not broke yet, but that's only a matter of time, and I don't want to take money from Andrew. Do you think it's a good idea to write for television?"

"Yes. A perfectly good idea. If you write your books as well."

"Oh, *Judith*. Anyone would think you had a part interest. In 'my books'. You still haven't told me, though, why it matters. Being a novelist isn't what one wants out of life. Or only incidentally : with someone who's really the important thing as your audience. Anyway, if you're a woman."

"I think it matters because people can only be one person. And somebody else's book might, oh, I don't know—lessen one's incomprehension?"

"Yes, but——"

"And from your point of view? Doesn't it matter because if you want to live 'fully' in the way you're fond of talking about, you must create something? You're lucky. You *can* write."

"There are a dozen easier ways to do it. There's the obvious way. For a woman." Her hesitation was just apparent. "Didn't you want to have a baby?"

"There were rather a lot of reasons——"

77

"With Martin." She nodded. "I suppose the *Channing*, in a way, is a bit like a child for you."

"I didn't create it."

"One doesn't create an adopted child. Not in simple terms. But all the same I imagine one *does;* one has created it."

I was looking at her, at the outline of her averted face.

Out of place, in advance of its time, it was one of those moments then which were to become an instrinic part of my relationship with her; moments when I ceased altogether to think of her as young.

She misinterpreted my silence. "Oh, I don't want to argue for the sake of it," she said. "I don't want to argue at all. Just one thing. One thing, Judith, tell me. You don't feel—do you?—life has any significance. Apart from whether we've liked it or not. You don't think there's anything for us outside 'having a good life'?—the way some old men say it before they die. 'Oh, well,' they say, 'I've had a good life.'"

"I don't know. Are you asking me if I'm religious? I don't think I am. I think one has to live life, either way, as though it's significant."

"Why?"

But I couldn't at once put into words just what it was I had meant.

"You mean," she said, "knowing you, the retreat in good order?"

This was so exactly it that I laughed; and experienced a feeling, suddenly, almost of elation. And of nearness to her, a feeling of the closest contact, so that I wanted to say her name.

78

After an instant, I drew her back against me.

The play didn't become interesting ; I doubt, anyway, if it could have interested me.

I began to be conscious of her hair ; her hair. Diana's. It was soft. It had the warmth of sun in it, the faintest human smell—and there was a moment when I touched it with my lips.

Given another chance to resist that act, with its irretrievable flicker of truth, I still don't think I could. There are such occasions.

She glanced round, half surprise in her look, I don't forget the surprise ; then she leant back closer into my arms.

I didn't know what she was thinking.

I found myself remembering the words ' *dure, vous savez, mais dure : si jeune* '. Bizarrely, ironically, they entered my mind. *Dure ?* Hardness the characteristic of youth ? Or rashness ? Emotionalism ? Eagerness for life ? . . .

I thought : what exactly am I doing ? Am I, as Margaret Carpenter said, being attracted ' in the right quarter ' ? Are you a homosexual ? Any kind of a homosexual ? Or am I just doing my best to make you one ?

I didn't say anything.

We watched the play to the end.

I didn't take her home.

II

Julian said about making up a four to go with Diana and Gerry to The Walnut that it was a very nice idea. " It would be still nicer, though," he said, " with just you."

But the four of us was to be the whole point.

It seemed to me probable, now, that I had revealed to Diana beyond denial a homosexual disposition. What I could deny, however, was any invitation—at best premature, since nothing relating to it had been rationally decided—to a love affair ; any lead into a life fundamentally outside society, at cross purposes with it. That lead I needn't give. On the contrary, could do the reverse : though without knowing, still, how seriously susceptible she was to any sort of sexual lead.

It was about ten when Julian and I reached Amory Street. The Walnut was much the same as clubs are: small and febrile, with its own particular taste, *flavour*, one either liked or didn't. There was a black band. A Spanish-Jamaican girl looked after the bar. She wasn't like most women with a job which is really to excite; she had no calculated, impersonal technique of provocation, and no hard shell. I had often been aware of her, and thought her attractive.

She smiled at Julian as we came in, and said good-evening.

Besides their tendency to irritate, perhaps all generalisations are practically valueless ; but it has seemed to me that if there is one thing more than another women

80

find sexually attractive in other women it is the idea of maternal tenderness in love.

Esther's smile had in it a suggestion of tenderness.

Not that on this occasion I noticed.

Julian had nodded pleasantly without going over to her. We were led to the table that had been reserved for us. He seemed almost too big for the route he was having to follow—his height emphasised in the crowded, confined space. He made his way with care, even cautiously. " Good," he said, as we sat down.

Diana and Gerry arrived soon afterwards.

Diana had just come from a party, and for the first time I saw her in evening dress. Her dress was ivory. She had bought it when her book had sold five thousand copies. She was too young for it, really, but her skin and her figure made nonsense of the criticism.

I was conscious immediately of the scent she was wearing ; it had the same sensual heaviness the smell of hyacinths has in a warm room, but the smell wasn't quite of hyacinths, it was of something manufactured and expensive, a commercial bid for delight.

Pinned improbably to her dress was a bunch of violets.

She met me with a look, a half smile, curiously sweet ; brief but unmistakably to remind me of the previous Sunday.

She said, seeming to do two things at once, " There were dozens of writers. What's wrong with Britain to-day, they said, is everyone's writing books and no-one's reading them. I felt quite guilty ; as if I was making it worse."

Gerry laughed.

I began to talk to Julian about the exotic murals, mostly landscapes, that had been painted all round the club. I talked to him, specifically to him, and listened, my eyes on his face, as he replied.

"Did you know 'wealh' is Old English for 'foreign'?" he asked. Conversationally he was rather like a good journalist : if it is true that a good journalist must know everything about something and something about everything. "Wealh Knut : Walnut. Perhaps there's method in the decor's madness."

"Though the proprietor's Portuguese."

"Mightn't he be a scholarly Portuguese?"

I nodded. "Perhaps."

I was aware of Gerry saying to Diana, "Why, look, that's France."

"Where? Let me see. Yes, it's the Dordogne." She had bent towards me to get a closer look at the painting on the wall behind us. "Heavens, I must go to France again."

"Who mustn't go to France again?"

I thought that Julian looked at me, rather, for the remark. "It's a lovely country," he said.

"Then that's a deal. Leave the stowawayage to me. We're off to Phila-ship's hold in the morning!"

Gerry's high spirits flowed over into an expansion of this nonsense.

And really, one could almost have imagined him ready to hitch at his trousers, make a gesture of throwing back what had been left of his reddish, cropped hair, and be off at once : vigorous, long-legged, lean.

Not that he had anything in common with the kind

82

of person whose enjoyment is always somewhere else, one step ahead. His enthusiasm included the present as readily as it did the future. The club was there for us to enjoy, and he got on uninhibitedly with the business of enjoying it.

I liked him. There was something warming and reassuring in his power to meet life more than half way. I don't think I ever knew anyone more gladly alive than he was.

He enjoyed Julian's choice of wines—though, despite persuasion, he had only a glass or so himself; he was in a rowing eight—as he enjoyed the hot rhythms of the band as he enjoyed Diana's perfume.

He was generously in love with Diana.

"But she's breaking my heart," he said, smiling at her. "I can't decide whether to kill myself, or make her jealous with the beautiful bar-maid."

"You won't get far with the beautiful bar-maid," Julian said.

"Why; have you tried?"

"She's married."

"Oh." Gerry didn't say it in so many words, but the sceptical face he made implied that perhaps, after all, bar-maids' husbands needn't be such an absolute impediment.

Julian caught his meaning. "She's devoted to her husband. They live in a bungalow in Harrow in a state of enviable domestic bliss. They collect bits of china to decorate the living-room. Their home is really very charming."

"We're to take it, then, she's not above a visitor or two?"

83

Julian laughed. " She was pretty hard pressed," he said, " some time ago, and I lent her a couple of pounds." The incident obviously struck him as too trifling either for concealment or development. " *They* most hospitably invited me to coffee. *They*. The husband's a very decent chap. An Australian. He's getting over T.B."

I knew that Diana was looking at me.

The band, unusually, was playing a fox-trot. I smiled at Julian, and said I would like to dance.

Gerry at once asked Diana.

She loved dancing.

He seemed to like best the dances he could dance with impatient, foot-tapping energy. He didn't bother much with the fox-trot ; just held her very close.

As they danced she met his gaze.

" Gerry, behave yourself," she said.

It was unbearable.

I tried to centre my attention on something else.

The young man with the band softly sang out his heart in a dateless dance song classic. ' Use your mentality . . .' he sang. ' Can't you see ? . . . it never can be. I'd sacrifice anything, come what might . . .'

He was a small, slight youth whose voice might have been spread with golden syrup. His name was Otto. Everything about him was so dainty he reminded me, after what Julian had said, of good china ; perhaps his own country's Dresden.

I remarked on this to Julian. Diana, who was dancing near us, overheard and smiled.

He was a part of the floor show. He sang night-club songs, innocently.

84

People appear sometimes to have resigned from sex ; even voluntarily, though that this is possible for ordinary people I find it so hard to believe. One could scarcely overlook it. There it is round every corner of life—the night-club or the street hoarding, the crying saxophone, the half-naked girl, it's just the same.

It had been on the tube that afternoon in the shape of two vivid, besotted Greeks, the young man intense and self-aware, the girl with a curious stupidity clouding her face, an air of being purchasable—and a marvellous sexual skill for leading him on.

Otto sang a song in French ; some delicately indecent song about a prince and his girl-friend.

Gerry laughed, and said to Diana, " I hope your French isn't very good."

" It's very good. But my French mistress never meant it for this."

People clapped.

Men looked at women.

Julian touched my arm, to say something.

And suddenly I experienced an overpowering desire to turn my back on all this, that made such an alien of me ; escape from it ; be free at least from the granite pressure of an external foreign normality into which I could never be absorbed.

The feeling wasn't new. Before, as often as not, I had gone from it to the Channing, work, impersonal routine. Now there was Diana.

I longed, now, to be just with her.

But the purpose of the evening was hardly to reveal that.

I asked Julian for more wine.

It was while we were watching the floor show that I first became aware of the American a few tables away. I suppose I noticed him because by then he had had enough to drink to become noticeable even in the crowded, noisy dimness of the club. He was alone ; perhaps bigger than Julian, square-chinned, and handsome in the way some Americans are. I realised he would be attractive to a lot of women. Presumably he realised it, too.

He looked continually in Diana's direction. (A great deal of life seems to go on in looks that people cannot, or anyway, do not amplify.) However, it wasn't until he was really drunk that he steered himself through the clinging, rhythmic couples over to our table, and asked her in a respectful Southern slur if she would dance with him.

She refused and, embarrassed, at a disadvantage because he was drunk, picked up her glass of wine in an effort to dismiss him ; as he bent down to repeat his invitation he staggered slightly against her, and wine from her glass spilt over the ivory dress.

He began to apologise.

I saw Gerry look at her, not with the self-concern of jealousy or awkwardness but with only sympathy for her in his face. It seems to me now like a flicker of his essential niceness in the dark of not knowing people ; never to be quite forgotten.

She managed a faint, unhappy smile before he got up and, making no more of it than a friendly chore, persuaded the drunk American towards the doorway.

Julian, after glancing in my direction, followed them.

86

Diana said, "Gerry——" And to me, "Will it be all right ? "

"Julian will see that it is.   He is the soul of discretion." I remember saying that.

" I don't know whether Gerry is or not.   Or the other man."   But she relaxed.   " Men certainly make life more exciting."

There was a pause ; she looked at me—and it was as if she had dropped some formal public act and was waiting for me to do the same.

" Are the violets too awful ? "

" You don't need them."

" But Gerry brought them.   He was carrying them in a big paper bag.   I had to wear them.   Do you mind ? "

" Of course I don't mind."

Then she said, her voice softening, " It would be nice if we were really here just on our own.   Wouldn't it ? "

Something in her look, as though knowing the way now, had gone straight to the source of my feeling for her.   If she wanted a reaction from me : the sudden deep fall of liquid emotion, the thrill, the physical weakening, she had what she wanted.

I thought : oh, darling, if you do this what's going to happen ?   What can you expect to happen ?

" He was quite a nice American.   Wasn't he ?   In his way."

I said, " Yes."

" I'll come and sit there.   It'll be easier to talk."

I had been sitting with Julian on the upholstered seat against the wall.

" In his way," she said again.   Her dress touched

87

mine. " Men want women, and women only want men to want them ? Who said that ? "

" I don't know. A poet, was it ? I shouldn't think it's much of the story."

She studied the stains on her dress. " I hope they come out. Does Chateau "—she looked at the bottle— " Climens come out ? I don't really like sweet wine as much as Julian was sure I should. Do you ? Though it's not so hard on the teeth as red." In the privacy of our nearness she took hold of my hand ; it might have been an ordinary, a quite natural thing to do. " Something always seems to happen to me when we're together. The first time we went out I practically broke my ankle." She laughed. " And that Sunday we went to see whatever it was and ' French——' "

She didn't finish what she was going to say : Julian and Gerry were back at the table.

" The gentleman agreed to a taxi," Julian said.

" He'd begun to look a bit green. He wasn't any trouble."

Gerry asked her about her dress.

I released myself from her hand.

When the next dance was over I made Julian sit with me again—yet feeling now that it was pointless ; that whatever elasticity of behaviour might or might not be possible in a normal woman emotionally face to face with another woman was neither here nor there, and that I was wasting my time trying to underline the vital, the practical precept : women are for men.

Julian said, " There's something I want to ask you, Judith."

88

Gerry drew back her chair for her. As she sat down he put his hands on her bare shoulders.

She said to Julian across the table, " You're creasing her dress."

Afterwards, when we were waiting for them to get the cars, she said, " I wish I was coming back with you."

" There's Gerry. Anyway, I've asked Julian in for a drink."

She didn't answer. For an instant I thought she was going to protest. She looked half puzzled and half distressed.

Then, " Good-night," she said, and lifted her face to be kissed before the others came back.

As if she had communicated anger to me, I thought all at once in anger : when you are in an impossible situation, how can you do anything else but make a mess of it ?

12

Julian and I sat in his car outside the flat. He said, " I wonder what you and your aunt would think about coming to France with me this summer ? I've been waiting to ask until I plucked up courage." He said this with a smile. " And until I had made sure I wasn't likely to end your days in a ' pile-up *anglais* '—being reluctant to harm a hair of two such elegant heads. You see, I thought we might take the car ; get down to Bandol, perhaps. I have a friend with a most pleasant

house on the coast there which will be empty except
for the housekeeper and her family. I think your aunt
would like it." He paused. " Or we could go wherever
you liked. Whenever you liked, for that matter. You
haven't arranged a holiday ? Your aunt hasn't, I know.
I think it could be a very agreeable time for the three of
us."

He made it sound agreeable. He remembered sun-
crusted hills, and thyme and lavender ; vineyards
and cicadas, and the sea, and the warm air ; the blue,
and pink, and peach-coloured houses ; flower markets
and food. He remembered his travel leaflets remorse-
lessly, and it had the same effect—the same easy emotional
force of a perfume, a look, or a dance song.

Only going to France without her now, or anywhere,
seemed like going into exile.

13

Two days later I received a small china figure. It was
of a boy. It was enchanting : the hands delicate, the
face downwards-looking, wistful. It reminded me,
though I couldn't recollect it well, of a Picasso painting
I had seen two or three years before—an early one of a
boy with his dove. The pastel shades were the same,
and there was something in the stance, a childishness, a
tenderness. With it came a note which said: ' I don't
know why, really—except that I don't much care for
Dresden. All my love, Diana.'

14

I didn't see her again until the celebration Andrew had at 'Four Winds' for his fifty-fifth birthday. I wrote to thank her for her present, and she telephoned me soon afterwards at the office. I said I would phone her back when we weren't so busy, but I hadn't done it.

I hadn't done anything, because I didn't know what I was going to do. I hadn't even achieved, as we sometimes do when put to it, a light, spurious sense of proportion. It was obvious that it mattered what I did now, if anything about human beings matters. I felt I was standing with my hand on the handle of a door, and wanted so much to open it, and believed I would be welcome, and was afraid to take the decision—though not for myself any more ; desire had ended that.

> '. . . the door we never opened
> Into the rose garden.'

Martin loved Eliot. The poem was one of his favourites.

I had liked it when he read to me.

I wondered : perhaps if there had never been anyone before Martin, no woman . . .

I went to 'Four Winds' not knowing what would happen there. I remember noticing the daffodils were at their peak, and about to fade.

She said, when the party had passed through its first access of congratulation and greeting, and there was a moment for us to talk, " Don't you like me any more ? "

91

Her voice was uncertain of itself; muted. Being busy is an excuse one offers in friendship perhaps, but not in love. " Do you always get tired of people so quickly ? "

" That's silly. Andrew will tell you how busy we've——"

" It doesn't matter."

Andrew, to be sociable, was explaining how Julian turned the society's books upside down. He stood among his guests, his black hair carefully brushed, his sallow-skinned, rather heavy face now wearing an expression of hard-bitten affability. I heard him say as Gerry came up to us, " Not that any fool can't read them the right way up, of course "—and Mrs. Rivers, who was younger than her husband, and had insisted on the party, laughed, and took Julian's arm, and affected to take his part, at the same time gazing provocatively at Andrew.

Andrew could be good with wives when it suited him. It suited him now, and in his own way he played up to her.

That this was going on I was aware at the very edge of my mind, indifferently, as one might be aware of some street intercourse between people one didn't know.

Gerry winked.

Evening dress more than any other clothes, I think, suited Gerry. The very blackness and formality seemed to bring into relief his energy, his vigorous warm-blooded-ness. It would have been easy to imagine him getting ready for the evening : shaving, humming to himself as he sat on the bed and did up his quickly-rubbed-over shoes, running a hand through his hair, a foreshadowing male gesture, before he was off in search of anything life offered—awake to his own youth and life's riches.

92

He smiled at Diana.

" Good-bye," she said, looking at me.

I hardly saw her then until the game. If I was in one place she went to another. The party fed on its own mood, and it was Derek Lawrence who suggested we should play whatever it was, I forget exactly, something that involved switching all the lights off except for the room we were in, and sending us from its pinkly-lit, polished luxury into the new darkness.

I managed not to go with him when Julian felt a way into one of the bedrooms, which was already full of party laughter. The rest was an accident, the kind that happens anywhere, and is likely in small houses : farther along the landing I came face to face with her.

She had gone off with Gerry but now she was alone. We looked at each other in the thin dark ; for an instant neither of us spoke. From quite near, somewhere in the garden, Gerry was calling her.

She swallowed, a small, brief movement which was just a sound—and tension on my side then melted into utter longing for her, the longing to hold her close, to be kissed by her, to say simply, ' I love you, I love you, it was only because I don't want to hurt you ; I only want you.' And I knew that I wouldn't resist the longing.

" Diana——"

" It's all right," she said, and there was bitterness in her voice, and something else, too, something I couldn't quite separate and name. " It's all right, I'm going."

I felt rather than saw her look. It was hot, near tears, I think ; unbearably involved.

She turned away.

" Darling——"

But if she heard she didn't look back. I stared at her as she ran off into the dark, downstairs, towards the voice calling her name.

" Judith——" Julian said.

They didn't come back before I left.

" Where have they got to ? " demanded Andrew. " That chap's too dead set on making off by half. This is my birthday, not a bloody garden party."

15

It was Andrew who told me later she had gone to Lincoln to stay with the Paleys. He told me the next Saturday morning, as we were sitting in his room going through mortgage forms. It had been true we were busy. We were supposed to have been a committee of three, but Lawrence hadn't turned up.

" He's in Paris." Andrew began searching through the papers on his desk. " Head's screwed on the right way, but I doubt he was born on a Saturday." He paused, and frowned into space, as if checking up with himself. " Saturday," he said again. He returned to his search. " She went up there a couple of days ago. Heaven knows if we're to have Paley in the family after all." He was still frowning. " Her mother should be here giving an eye to things."

I didn't reply.

" Paley's entirely the wrong chap for her," he went on

94

then. "He's nothing but a young fool. Even if she wasn't years too young to be thinking of anything of the sort. Though what I'm supposed to do, I don't know. If she's made up her mind she's in love with him."

"Is she in love with him?"

"You tell me. But if it makes the place seem a bit empty not having her in it, it's certainly made it seem small lately having her about. Isn't that love? An uncomfortable thing to house? What else would you suggest?" He found the letter he was looking for. "Anyway, myself I'd rather see an end to the whole thing. She'll pay to-morrow for being a fool to-day. Besides,"—he handed me the letter—"I don't care for the boy. I don't see what good he can possibly do her. She's got a home here as long as she wants it. Women get altogether too worked up about love. Don't use their sense. Present company excepted, of course." He waved the letter, which I hadn't taken. "Judith, this is rather up your street. Selling at four thousand three hundred, buying five thousand three hundred, three thousand wanted on the two of them for paying off with interest when the sale's gone through. Harpenden. If the spirit moves you to visit your aunt, you might take a look at them; just a glance."

I read the letter.

Leave it, now. Leave her to go with the tide if she could—as I should have left her from the beginning.

As if there is anything sensible about love. Or its beginning—

As I was leaving the office Betty Shaw looked up at me from her desk. She had come in to do some typing

95

for us. She said, " Tom's giving up the navy. So we can be together."

I looked at her. She was so happy.

" Betty, have you finished Mr. Rivers' letter ? "

She coloured.

" It will be very nice for you. For both of you," I added, ashamed.

Poor Betty : Miss Bowyer, and me.

I asked her if she would telephone my hairdresser's. At that moment it was solely to convey friendliness again.

But I wanted to cancel my next week's appointment. The appointment was on Julian's birthday—and he had said that what he would like for his birthday was to come to dinner at the flat.

He came.

And was nice about the dinner : which I had prepared with absurd concentration, as if (Jean-Pierre had told me in an uncharacteristic moment how he did his steak) piercing certain herbs into the meat and splashing it with brandy was all there was of consequence in life. I scarcely noticed the result. I remember he tried to make me change my mind about France. We were having our coffee before he mentioned that he had seen Diana the previous night. He had seen her at ' Four Winds '. She was back from Lincoln.

" How was she ? "

" She seemed all right. She doesn't play bridge, apparently." He sounded entirely unengaged, as if we could just as well have made after-dinner conversation to each other on almost any other topic as on this one. He had pushed his chair back slightly from the table.

96

"A good deal of the evening she spent by herself—somewhat exceptionally, I gather—flirting with cigarettes in odd corners. Perhaps she was thinking up her next chapter."

"Yes."

"Anyway, it's a nice thought," he said, his tone changing a little. "She's written one delightful book, and she's nineteen, and personally charming, so in keeping with the times she's been made a lot of fuss of for it. But I doubt if all the attention's helped. In her case, especially."

"Why in her case, especially?"

"Temperament apart?" He drank some more coffee. "Well, her life could hardly be said to abound in steadying influences. As far as one can see. I wouldn't say Paley's a steadying influence. Would you?"

"What did she say about him?"

"I don't think she said anything about him."

"Don't you think he's the right person for her?"

"The right person," he repeated. "Well, who is to say who's the right person for us—except ourselves? He's a nice enough boy. I would have thought his attitude to life was a little over-simple. Or over-simplified—he's not a fool. It's a characteristic of a good many young scientists. But is she likely to marry him, though? If that's what you meant."

"Andrew thinks so." I paused. "He thinks she might."

"Isn't she more likely to look for someone not just less, well, vagrant perhaps, mutable, in temperament

97

than she is herself but someone better able to hold her
something like steady. I should have thought she would
look, consciously or unconsciously, for some sort of
stability. I don't know, of course. I only know what
I see."

"She didn't stay in Lincoln long."

He shook his head. "Of course, her television
programme's on——"

A knock at the door interrupted him.

Without any idea who it might be, I went into the
hall. For some reason, I thought of Martin.

However, Helen on the doorstep looked expected.
"I'm sorry I'm late," she said. "I was so hungry
I went straight and had a meal. Bits on toast never did
fill me. How are you? Heavens, it's nice to be here."

Because it was Helen I was spared embarrassment, but
not a sense of abysmal, inexcusable carelessness.

She took off her hat, ruffled up her hair quickly in
front of the hall glass, and went with a show of pleasure
and without fuss into the room where Julian was sitting.
"The bridesmaids looked charming in delphinium tulle,"
she said.

At the sight of him she seemed to change into a quite
different person. She had been at home, pleased to see
me again, unthinkingly confident in the sexless familiarity
of our friendship—which had lasted since our first days
together at a new school. She became quite different.

"Well——!" she said, on a pointless note of implica-
tion and astonishment.

She and Julian hadn't met.

He stood up, courteously, and let the explanations

98

about her wedding, and himself, and my regrets for my stupidity drop round him as if they were something innately pleasant. Again, it was a situation to emphasise his height—and his male good looks, his nicely-manicured masculinity. But if he wasn't lost on her, her manner did what it could to convey that he was. She had taken to protecting herself with that.

"Well, and here I was looking forward to a cosy chat," she said. "All girls together."

We hurried to drinks.

She accepted her second with, "I will, thanks. I have, as you know, a tendency to finish the bottle not uncommon among old maids." Though she laughed as she said it, it didn't help.

For the sake of saying something, Julian said, "Weddings are in the air. Violet Ammersgate is next." She had succeeded in making him uncomfortable.

I don't think he was sorry when the telephone rang. He went to answer it. It was my aunt, and he stayed talking to her.

Getting up, Helen went over to the bookshelves, where Diana's china boy was. She examined it as she walked, fidgeting, about the room. "Pretty," she said finally. "It's new. Where——?"

Julian said good-bye to my aunt.

She put the figure on the little table between the armchairs, and waited for him to come back into the room. A moment later he had knocked it off on to the floor.

My love for Diana suddenly in my throat, I watched the small, ominous mime. Then they bent down together, united in the fear of having broken what is somebody else's.

It wasn't broken. It lay on the carpet intact; the limbs, the minute fingers intact.

Helen laughed, in an aftermath of relief and naturalness which once again transformed her.

They began to apologise to me, both of them claiming the blame.

Julian said, "I am too big and awkward for this hazardous, lady's flat."

He smiled at her.

I didn't see but imagined her pleasure as I went to the phone.

She said after he had gone that she had liked him, and didn't add anything to this; or nothing sharp-edged and protective.

"He was wearing a nice tie. Did you notice? Quiet, but nice. Blue. A lovely shade of blue. It went beautifully with his shirt."

"I think he really does *choose* his ties. I can always imagine him in some quiet, superior shop weighing one against the other."

"I thought he dressed very well. I don't care for the arty-crafty type. He has a rather athletic sort of figure, though. Don't you think? It was almost as if he were shut up in his clothes, poor lamb."

I looked at her.

It seemed a man's smile of alliance could make this much difference.

How difficult on the whole it is to imagine states of desire at odds with one's own experience, and therefore touched with incredibility. I found it so hard to believe in hers, really believe in it, that I half believed some

100

pretence must be involved; though I knew that it wasn't.

"Helen, you remember what you said once about Miss Dennis—that women like that defeated you?"

She said yes, surprised—seeing, I suppose, no reason for my question at that point in the conversation, no logical ' tie-up '. However, I went on, "All other considerations aside, would it be *possible* for you to get any pleasure out of making love to a woman? I mean with someone attractive, you loved; liked."

She stared at me.

"Or does the whole idea simply——?"

"I couldn't bear it," she said. "Whatever made you think of that?"

"I just wondered. I just thought, suddenly, why shouldn't women's physical attractiveness attract women as well as men."

"I think men are much more physically attractive. There's some point in a man."

When I next saw Julian he said he thought she was the kind of person one would have to know very well to know at all. "She is at great pains to conceal herself."

"Isn't that true of everyone?"

"Perhaps ; but I felt, towards the end of the evening, she is so much nicer than she wants people to think. I liked her. And in a way I think I was rather sorry for her ; she seemed to me as if she wouldn't make friends easily."

"She makes friends with women quite easily."

"Oh," he said.

"If you like her, why don't you take her out somewhere

101

when she comes to stay in the summer?" I made the suggestion by chance, hardly thinking about it; magnanimous with what was of no account. "She likes you."

"Oh, I didn't mean——" He stopped. "Do you want me to?"

"She'd enjoy it."

"Well, if it would be any satisfaction to her, or to you, I will, of course. I was once told by a woman I knew that men are intolerably selfish in their social behaviour. It struck me at the time as rather true."

"It's the last thing I would have said, so far as you're concerned. You could telephone her one evening at the flat."

"Then I will."

He made a neat note in his pocket-book of the week in July.

16

The television programme was latish, almost ten. When at the end of it she hadn't appeared I telephoned 'Four Winds'. We are perhaps curious about those who are unimportant to us; one is easily made afraid for somebody one loves.

There was no reply. Andrew, I knew, had arranged to spend the week-end in Glasgow.

I tried to get through to Gerry, at the flat where he stayed in London. A voice said, a man's voice,

"He isn't here. I believe he's gone off for the week-end."

I tried 'Four Winds' again.

After that I could only wait for to-morrow, which was Violet Ammersgate's wedding.

She was marrying a navy chaplain. Andrew wasn't going. When it came to a wedding or a business deal, I dare say he had no difficulty in making his choice. Nobody had said whether Diana would be or not, and I hadn't asked : an irrational part of me half hoping, I suppose, to see her, but only by chance. It was probably assumed that I knew, anyway. There was no reason why a falling-off of our friendship should be attributed by such other people as were even aware of it to anything in the nature of a break ; to anything more, in fact, than a natural developing on her part of interests elsewhere.

Both Martin and I had been invited. Violet had always liked Martin ; and she had telephoned me to ask if the two of us at the same wedding would distress each other. It was nice of her, but not necessary. He had tickets for a theatre afterwards. They were for a play he said we would especially enjoy together.

In the morning it poured with rain, and we went in the car to fetch my aunt.

The church was a village church in Hertfordshire. The rain had just stopped when we arrived there, and a washed-out sun ran over the grey stones. The smell of age and consecration which met us at the porch was mixed with the smell of weddings, a smell of make-up and celebration.

The organ began with the loud suddenness of music

103

beginning in churches, and an almost tangible response to it seemed to stir round the pews, which were very full.

The bride came into the church.

The words of the service, words her father spoke as if he had long ago grown bored by them, had an impregnable poetry.

" '. . . And forsaking all other keep thee only unto her,' " he said.

Martin glanced at me ; a moment later I saw Diana.

She seemed to be alone. She saw me, and looked back without smiling, without turning away. Her face was pale, shadowy, against her lipstick's fresh brilliance. She had a flower pinned to her suit. Her suit was a black skin of velvet, her hat adamantly gay.

" What are you looking at ? " Martin said.

People began to kneel.

Afterwards I couldn't see her any more in the crowd pausing and hesitating its way to the door. It was outside, when we were held up by the photographers and everyone stood about talking, that I heard Ammersgate ask, " *Where* did you get to last night ? We turned on, of course, and then there wasn't a sign of you. Whatever happened ? "—and saw that he was talking to her.

" Nothing happened," she said. " Only I'm not writing a book any more. So I couldn't talk about what I'm not doing. Could I ? It would have been false pretences, and a waste of time."

" Not writing any more ? "

" I've given it up," she said, and laughed, without much amusement. " I've decided it's like love : not

104

worth what it takes. Though perhaps one shouldn't say such things at weddings."

She turned to me. "Judith. It's nice to see you again."

I asked her how she was.

"Incredibly tired." Her tone had a social sheen. "I've come from Lincoln this morning."

She went on to say something or other polite to my aunt.

My aunt had come to the service because of the Ammersgates, but she had excused herself from the reception. As Martin and I were saying good-bye to her I saw Diana go off in Derek Lawrence's car.

She was still with him at the reception.

She didn't seem to be drinking a lot as wedding receptions go, but she was drinking too much for someone who was tired and eating nothing. She had an overtone of excitement to her voice when we arrived. After a little while she quietened this, as if she had suddenly caught the sound of it herself; but she didn't stop accepting the drinks she was being offered.

And when she did, it seemed that it was too late, that the confusion creeping up on her alcoholic glow had been abrupt and treacherous.

Lawrence watched her, half smiling.

The two things I knew about him were that he was clever, and that he liked what he obstinately called 'living it up'. I had heard Betty Shaw describe him once as 'a bachelor gay who had gone on too long'. This had seemed to me rather unfair, since I don't think he was more than about thirty. However, she knew

105

him better than I did. His stated preference was for teen-age girls.

He said, " Are you doing anything afterwards, Diana ? Would it amuse you to have dinner with me ? "

" I'm going to Pat's." Her voice now had begun to have a kind of opaque warmth.

" To Pat's ? Who is Pat ? Perhaps I could take you there ? "

" I'm going to Pat's to stay the night."

" Perhaps we could get there a little late ? "

" I don't know," she said mildly.

" Not really. Diana's promised to come with us."

She looked at me in surprise—and didn't say anything.

" What, are we going ? " Martin said.

She sat on the seat between us in the car, her thigh forced against mine. Ammersgate had shut the door, but too delicately, so that it hadn't double-locked. Martin leant over and gave it a slam. I loved him for the slam. " All cosy, girls ? " he said.

I asked, " Where does Pat live ? I can't remember the address."

" I don't know."

Martin said, " What about some coffee for everyone ? I'll make some coffee if you'll come back home."

Her eyes were very bright.

" Do you mind if we go to Martin's flat first ? "

" Why should I mind ? " she said. " I only came to the wedding to see you."

Martin had been saying that ' flat ' *was* a better word ; his glance at this implied that she must be very drunk.

It seemed a long way to London. At first she talked

a good deal without any very clear idea of what she was saying ; then with the miles the glow began to fade.

After Martin's brutal ebony coffee, which he gave to her in large cupfuls, she sat still and white-faced in one of the armchairs. Her skirt was marked with some drops of coffee she had spilt.

She said, " I'm sorry. I didn't mean to make a nuisance of myself. I've done quite enough of that already."

He smiled at her, standing by the fire-place playing with an Egyptian head we had once bought together. The head sprang up from a lotus. It had seemed important at the time that we should have both thought it beautiful ; that he should have been able to tell me the lotus in Ancient Egypt symbolised the sun. I had learnt since that such things are only of relative importance.

" I'm ruining your evening."

" That's for us to say."

" I'll go now." She stood up, putting an arm against her forehead and brushing back her hair.

" Don't you want a cigarette ? " Months ago I had begun to buy the cigarettes I knew she liked, and had gone on getting them.

" Oh." She hesitated, and touched one from the packet. For the first time she looked directly at me.

I said, " We'll take you to Pat's."

" If you're late for your theatre as well as——"

" We shan't be late."

I suppose something must have been mentioned earlier

about the theatre. I don't remember. Anyway, Martin showed her the tickets. " There, you see : lots of time," he said.

But in the end she didn't come with us. She said she thought, after all, she would rather go on to Pat's by herself later. " I'll get a taxi. Will it be all right if I just sit here and have one more cigarette ? "

Her cigarette end burned on some ash and cinders left in the grate.

" As far as I'm concerned," Martin said, his laugh brief, " you can stay here all night."

" You won't get a taxi very easily."

" I don't mind walking."

It was because Martin forgot the tickets that I went back to his flat. " No, I'll go," he said ; but it was too easy to disregard him and return to her.

I stood at the door and felt for the key still in my purse. The thought of her sitting as we had left her was like pain ; only going back could begin to stop it.

I found her in tears, her face pressed against the hard, cold back of her chair. She didn't look up, or answer me. My return at that moment was unmanageable, and she acknowledged it.

After a further attempt I made her look at me.

" What's the matter ? "

She freed herself.

" What's the matter ? "

" Nothing."

" That's silly."

" Well then, everything." Everything : the easy excuse for more specific grief. " Nothing's any use that

108

I do. There isn't any sense in anything." The very childishness of the words sharpened my pity.

We hadn't long. Martin was in the car downstairs. "There doesn't seem to have been much sense in last night. Or in to-day." I heard that I was speaking less gently than I had meant to.

"You don't know about last night."

"You can tell me."

"I went with Gerry. To a pub a friend of his has. In Sett. We stayed the night there." She had stopped crying : her voice suddenly sounded quite flat. "It seemed as if it might be romantic or something—on the spur of the moment and leaving everything behind. Something drastic was needed to make it romantic. Sett's a very romantic village. But it wasn't."

"To sleep with Gerry?"

"Yes. But we had before." She looked at me. "The first time was Andrew's party."

I felt no surprise. I didn't know what it was that I felt : anger or jealousy or regret ; what it was.

"Didn't you——?" The question was an impossible one to ask.

But she understood. "Didn't it come up to expectations?" she said. "Oh, well ; but the motions are meaningless without the chemicals."

Silent, I picked up the tickets from the table.

She said, watching me, "Please go, Judith. You can't help it."

"No. Exactly what can't I help?"

"That I thought you cared about me. Only you don't. I mean, that I thought I was important to you,

109

that it was both of us. I've been very stupid. I don't want to be any stupider."

I heard Martin get out of the car.

"Diana, listen. Go to the flat. Phone Pat that you're not coming. I'll get home as soon as I can."

I left her my key.

I didn't know if she would come to me or not.

Martin and I met on the stairs.

As we came out of the theatre he took my arm. "That was marvellous," he said. "Exciting. When you get comedy played by a tragedienne, a French one at that, it gives a kind of excitement to the whole thing." We walked along the pavement, not going anywhere in particular. "Or perhaps it was being with you. I don't normally react to theatre-going with excitement. I do everything too often; live the life, in fact, of someone in his twenties—his bachelor twenties." He laughed. "It's the envy of half my married colleagues."

I tried to think of something to reply.

He gave me the chance, and when I couldn't went on, "I suppose most men would be in their dotage before they married for anything except a woman."

"Perhaps. I don't know enough about men."

"Their over-all objectives are less crystallised than women's; that's one thing. They're less sure half the time what's good for them." He flicked his cigarette, and the end of hot ash broke up and blew brilliantly about. "I wish I thought filters were the slightest use. Only marriage creates a genuinely adult *climate*. While we're on the subject. A climate of stability. Affairs don't. If they're stable, it's in spite of themselves.

110

Only marriage, in a sense, stands still. Don't you think so ? "

We had come near to the corner of Shaftesbury Avenue. Two girls passed by, and glanced at him, at his brown, masculine face, as we began to walk slower.

" Well," he said. There was a pause. " One of those looked a bit like Diana. Now there's an idea. Should I marry our hard-drinking little delinquent ? At any rate she wouldn't be, an unrelieved monotony. That reminds me of something. Auden. Art is not life and cannot be, a something or other to society. Midwife. Isn't it ?—fundamentally. And can't it be ? She's interesting for her age. Would she marry me, do you think ? "

" You will have to ask her."

" That's the trouble, though : I never do. I'm not sure I ever feel entirely de-married." The smile I expected didn't come ; or barely came. " Probably it's that there isn't any one else, for either of us. To marry, I mean. Marriages that go down the drain between more or less possible people must ninety times out of a hundred be because of someone else."

" Yes. I should think so."

" Someone else clinches it. Whatever other things there might have been, a divorce judge by himself isn't destiny." Then he smiled. " Well, what are we going to do, Judith ? Apart from be lone wolves to the end. Something to eat ? "

I looked at him. " If you don't mind, Martin, I think I'll go home. I'm rather tired."

" Oh. Must you ? "

111

" Too many late nights."

" Of course, if you're tired——"

I left him with his urge to talk, about himself, about us, unsatisfied.

Love has it in it to be a narrow, unrelenting compulsion.

She was waiting for me almost in the dark, the small lamp brightening her hair.   On the table there was a dish of cereal she must have got for herself and then not eaten.   Her face had the poignant drabness of exhaustion and past tears.

" I wasn't going to.   Still, I've done what you said. You'd have been locked out if I hadn't."

Absurdly, I hadn't considered being locked out.

" I'm sorry it was only that."

" Did you like the play ? "

" Yes.   But I shan't like it if you try to talk to me about it."

" What else can we do ? " she said quickly.   " When you don't want—if you don't want what it was before."

" What I don't want is for you to be unhappy."   I sat down on the settee.   " What would make you happy ? "

" I don't know."

" Think."

" Being with you.   Only if you wanted it."

" I've never not wanted it.   There've been other things, but not that.   Never mind them.   Would it do in France ? "

She looked at me.

" Would it be nice being together in France ?   What have you done about a holiday ? "

She was still silent.

Then suddenly she smiled. " Is it happening to me ? " she said. " This sort of thing doesn't. Does it ? Yes, please. Oh, Judith, yes, please." It was with a kind of awkwardness that she touched my cheek.

There was nothing further in the way of emotional inquests. She began to tell me how much money she had still, and that she hadn't paid yet for a fur jacket she had bought as a present for her mother. " But I shall be getting some more," she said. " And we needn't stay in desperately expensive hotels, need we ? As soon as I can I'll finish what I'm writing now."

She didn't say any more about not being a writer.

But she said something about Martin and money. As we were getting ready for bed she asked me, abruptly, an abrupt switch from anything that had gone before, if he paid me any sort of allowance. " For being divorced."

" No, of course not. It wasn't like that. Why ? "

" I don't know," she said. " I'm just glad he doesn't, that's all. I wouldn't have liked him to. Though I like Martin. I didn't think I was going to, but I do." She paused. " He's nice. He has a nice mouth. If I were anyone else, I should think it would be nice to be kissed by him." Again there was the pause. " Judith, will you ever go back to him ? "

" No. I won't go back to him."

We looked at each other ; that was all. There was time now.

She began to examine her skirt ; when she spoke again it was to say that coffee stained worse than Château Climens.

113

That night I could hear her from my room if she moved. I didn't go to her.

At the back of my mind was the small reservation that when we made love, the first unmistakable move towards it, however uneasy, however young, should come from her ; that she should want it, should want me, enough for that. I didn't imagine this was of any practical significance. I was quite sure that she would. I was quite sure now that we should make love : so sure that I suppose it had something in it of a decision.

I didn't know when, when the moment would come, or how it would all end ; but I awaited it as one might a honeymoon of which only the date remains to be decided : without intolerable impatience, not as the beginning and end all of the relationship, yet with a sense of almost breathless delight.

There were different things. There was a relief, curiously detached and mental, that now at least— within the framework of our situation—we could behave as adults and not over-emotional schoolchildren. A deep inescapable knowledge of the *significance* if not the wrong of what, inwardly, was already accepted. But these things, everything else I felt and knew, were contained in and dominated by the new glowing apprehension of sexual joy.

When eventually I went to sleep I dreamt that I was kissing her.

114

Part Two

I

" Didn't Julian mind ? "

" Well, he's lent us some good maps for someone who did."

" Won't he need them himself? "

" He isn't coming until after we get back."

" We're not going to use maps, are we ? I would have minded if you hadn't come with me."

I took off my sun-glasses. The day's glare was over. " I think he believed really I was afraid of gossip. You know the sort of thing. ' Will they or won't they ? ' "

" Will they or won't they what ? "

" Don't be silly."

She giggled. " It might have made people think you were going to *marry* Julian. Even your aunt wouldn't have saved you from that."

" No. All the same it wasn't the reason I didn't go with him."

France's first sensual impact was behind us. We had left the port behind, with its atmosphere of half-drugged busyness in the hot, smoky afternoon sun ; its line of motionless boys looking and fishing ; its smell —overpoweringly to do with food.

We had had final salutes from French port officials, and driven cautiously from the quay under the protection of all the other cars doing the same. Seen our first English accident at the side of the road, and been waved

117

on by a stylish gendarme. Felt a kind of singing holiday ecstasy, almost an exultation, at the stretches of June countryside waiting for us.

It was she who put the ecstasy into words, eagerly upright at my side.

There had been a French car with its registration number written on in heliotrope chalk which made her laugh, and English cars with occupants going home who hooted and waved to us because of our GB and put a light to the excited sociability of her mood.

Now the first gushes of sensation had subsided—and soaked in pleasure we drove without resolution towards the Dordogne.

We had no plans worth the name. Our day or so of preparation had included essentials, and one or two inessentials : for instance, her complicated picnicking stove. But no plans. It was by chance that we stayed our first night at Farville. We simply stopped driving when we were tired of it.

I remember Farville, an unremarkable small northern town, as the bright morning of a period when once more being together, on our own, unhurried, and (or so it seemed) beyond the reach of our ordinary lives was like standing in a flood of full sunlight which blotted out before and afterwards and was enough in itself. During that period, now that it had come—and it appeared to me as some kind of emotional phenomenon—I was conscious of no further desire than to be with her ; I had no feeling of sensual deprivation, and none of impatience.

When I went to her room in the hotel to see if she was

118

ready for dinner I found her lying on the bed in a dressing-gown, her arms folded under her head.

She had become quieter in mood, but not less obviously gay. She said, " I'm more ready than I look. Though bidets, I think, are something one should take up in early childhood. Are you persuasive with a bidet, or do you dominate it? "

" Do you mean am I personally, or should one be? Diana, your dress is lovely."

She got up, and took her dress from its hanger. Her dressing-gown or something about her smelt of the hyacinth scent. " I shall sit in the bar and sip beautifully and hope to be looked at. It's nice being looked at in France. They're so interested. Not that they really care the first thing about you. If you were piebald and lived with a lizard, they wouldn't really *care*. They might make French remarks."

" They might."

" I've decided about Frenchmen it's absinth and what it does to their frontal lobes. If you interfere with monkeys' frontal lobes they sit on each other."

" Individualism could hardly go farther."

" Did you know? That they sit on each other? "

" I don't think I did."

" I expect you'd rather have your frontal lobes left alone. Though you'd probably be better without some of them." She laughed. " I wouldn't. I couldn't bear to have my *ears* pierced. I think the French are on better terms with the realities of life than we are. Don't you? Do they polish their floors with absinth? "

" After they've had their dinner."

119

"I'm *sorry*, darling, I'm just coming. Anyway, I love them and their floors and whatever they polish them with. Oh, Judith, I love being back. Absinth makes the heart grow fonder." She laughed at herself, and turning to me suddenly put her arms round my neck. " Perhaps even my wallpaper will turn out to be an acquired taste."

She released me.

The wallpaper in the dining-room had a plot. The little girl at the next table studied the pictures of picnics and lovers with the incredible gravity and dignity of small French children.

At the table next to her were two elderly English women who went firmly to have their coffee outside when the time came, though now there was quite a wind. As they passed her one of them said in uneasy French, " Aren't you a pretty little girl ? "

She gravely and politely shook her head.

" What's your name ? "

" Nadine."

The parents ignored the incident, and talked about them with light contempt afterwards.

Diana had interestedly observed it all. " Two of the world's unclaimed treasures," she murmured.

" Do you make French remarks, too, when you're in France ? "

" No. I take it back. I'm inalienably English and sentimental and unrealistic. An eccentric old maid is the perfect thing to be."

These words, then, couldn't pierce my happiness ; though they led me to smile at her : and hold her responding smile. " I thought you were a tough character."

120

" That was once."

" Why once ? " I wanted the answer.

But she said, " It must be in the blood. Perhaps I take after Andrew." Then she went on, chattering, one thing having led to the next, " You know, Judith, Andrew really did make a row over Sett and Gerry. Though he didn't know everything, of course. As if it was especially Gerry's fault. I talked a lot of nonsense to Gerry, and I wouldn't have taken any notice if he'd argued, anyway. Besides, he isn't my keeper. But to listen to Andrew you'd have thought he was. You'd have thought his whole mission in life was my future."

" Oh."

" Or ought to have been. Future's such a funny word when anyone actually uses it. Isn't it ? I suppose the real reason Andrew was furious was the publicity that got passed up. After all, he had persuaded that T.V. man along. I tried to talk to him, but he wouldn't talk. He just kept blaming everything on Gerry. Gerry was the uncaring villain. He more or less threw him out of ' Four Winds '. And Gerry lost his temper, and I don't wonder, and said ' What the hell.' " She paused, and looked at me. " And now I'm with you. And I think Andrew was quite glad. About you and France. I don't think he was sure what was to be done about me next. And here we are. And, oh, Judith—what a lovely dinner we've had ! The first one is always the best."

" All this," I said, " for——" And I tried to work out the bill.

" Oh, no. Not all this for that. I may not be the business woman, but I know what you can buy."

121

The next day, early, I heard her singing to herself outside in the yard as she examined her stove. Her voice when she sang was very soft and light, and rather high ; utterly feminine. It had a caressing quality not normally there. It made me imagine her momentarily with a child. Even this, at Farville, resulted in a strange, sharp kind of pleasure.

When she saw me she called up, " It's a most heavenly day. We'll go hundreds of miles to-day, shall we? Shall we picnic in a wood ? "

It took us one more night to reach Mirrepont. We stayed the night at a rather primitive, poetic-looking village inn in Haut-Vienne—not because we particularly wanted to but because we had been caught unawares by the distances there can be between the towns.

The village itself was in the hands of an early travelling fair. The woman who ran the inn called the fair ' ma fortune '. " *Mais ce sera tout fini vers onze heures,*" she lied as she showed us rooms looking out on to the square.

By eleven o'clock a dance that had started in the local hall was spilling out all over the square, and loud, distorted gramophone music from it was competing with music from the sideshows, and from the children's roundabout. The roundabout revolved decorously and tirelessly at the centre of things to three obstinate, out-of-date tunes. Wedged vehicles hooted. French families of fat men and fat, down-to-earth women, purposeful youths and girls in dark, tight skirts and high heels all shouted at once. Only the small children were silent with their revolving delight.

The square was a great breathing lung of noise.

122

Diana watched the scene from my window-ledge, fascinated : until eventually a protesting, thick-voiced drunk stumbled by the hotel, and broke the spell.

She gazed after him as he continued his unsafe way out of sight, bumping against the walls of the houses, lurching perilously towards the kerb. Then she said, looking round at me, and grimacing suddenly, " Heavens, Judith, *I* wasn't anything like that ; was I ? "

" No, darling—nothing."

" But I'd drunk too much. I don't remember bits of it clearly. I remember you were terribly annoyed."

" Was I ? "

" Have you ever been drunk ? "

" Yes. More or less. Hasn't everyone ? "

" I mean, for a long time."

" Oh, hours and hours." I laughed at her. " Well, I don't make a practice of it."

" Why ? No, not why don't you make a practice of it. Don't you ever want to drink ? Don't you want to drink—oh for the state of the world ? "

" I should think it's the last thing it would help."

" What do you think about people drinking ? "

" Oh, Diana. I don't know. Do I think anything about it ? More than the obvious."

" Why were you angry with me ? Why didn't you want me to drink ? "

" You ? Oh. Perhaps because women are vulnerable when they drink. Well, *vulnerable*. I mean, at any rate it's better that they should know what it is they're doing. Being young, and adorable, makes them seem vulnerable."

123

"Am I adorable? How nice. What is the most adorable thing about me?"

I was standing near her.

She looked at me, smiling, waiting for a reply. Our eyes met.

I lifted her face and turned it a little, regarding it. "Now I don't know. Yesterday I would have said your voice."

"Voice?"

"When you were singing it was like—I thought it was like distilled Eve."

"It's a nice phrase. Can I borrow it? Before or after the apple?"

"Does it matter?"

"Your face is like after the apple. Not new. Oh, I don't mean old." Quickly, she laughed. When she said 'I love your face', her tone had changed.

For a moment we seemed to stand very still.

Please kiss me now, I felt; please want me.

There was a pause, but then she said, turning away, "Let's go and join in. It's the only thing to do. And, anyway, it would be fun."

"Do you think so?"

"Yes. Come with me, Judith," she said. "Do that for me—just that."

I thought her words odd, not knowing yet what she meant by them.

She dragged me at once out into the square.

We ended the night dancing with French boys in American shirts.

It was just four as we climbed the thin flights of stairs

124

to our landing. Close by the door of the hotel there had been a man of about fifty, slim and tall, with a mauvish face and spare, oiled hair—he is still very vivid to me— who held a girl of perhaps fourteen or fifteen in his arms. He wasn't talking to her, just holding her in his arms and boldly caressing her.

He was the end of all my content. I felt against him a flash of hatred which was ridiculous against someone I didn't know ; or someone I did know. And for her, for Diana, I felt without warning a sudden new unbearable intensity of physical desire.

" I'm dying to clean my teeth," she said, stopping on the stairs to glance down at me. " Judith, that pink stuff ! "

Our rooms now seemed rather worse than they had done earlier. I pulled my bed away from the cracked wall. I had an iron bedstead. I could hear her washing. Our bidets were tins on rickety stands.

After a little while she came in to me.

" I thought I'd better tell you," she said. " There are a lot of black beetles you won't like in the lavatory. They've come out from under the skirting-board." Then as I stood staring at her she added, with composure, with mildness almost, and a surpassing delicacy, " Of course, one has to expect a certain amount of something of the sort when one's on holiday."

She kissed me good-night rather briefly. She didn't stay to talk.

In an hour or so the room through its wobbly, faded shutters was streaked with shadow and early morning sun. Somewhere a cement-mixer had started.

125

Next door I found her feeding a surprised-looking cat with sweet biscuits.

That was the day we had her picnic in a wood ; or on the edge of a wood. It was as we were going into it afterwards that we realised we were being shouted at by a blue-overalled man on a bicycle.

Most of what he was shouting angrily in country dialect I couldn't understand, but it was clear that he didn't want us to go into the wood.

We paused, and he got off his bicycle and came walking towards us.

" Foreigners here should keep to the roads," he said, very loudly and slowly, coping with fools. He said it twice.

I said, " If the wood is private, of course——"

" There are snakes in the wood."

Immediately he walked back to his bicycle, and put a contemptuous leg over the saddle.

He was a disagreeable-looking man. He had a coarse face, and a thick, black moustache ; his walk had been curiously bullying. But suddenly Diana called after him, and thanked him for telling us about the snakes, and asked him if he would help us finish the bottle of vin rosé we had been drinking.

He came back.

However, he wasn't much pleasanter as a companion than one might have imagined ; and afterwards I asked her why she had done what she had.

" Well, he needn't have bothered ; need he ? And, anyway, I didn't want him, not even him, to go off like that." She threw away the end of her cigarette, and smiled at me. " I'm too happy."

126

" Are you happy ? "

" Yes."

" Completely ? "

" Yes." If there had been a pause, it was too slight for one to be sure.

We drove south, finding ourselves flanked suddenly by yoked oxen, and a whitewashed domestic simplicity that was hard to believe in but touched, in passing, with beauty.

" What are you thinking about ? "

She said, " I was trying to think how I could have made a joke about modesty going by the ' bord '. "

We reached Mirrepont.

She was delighted by Mirrepont ; by the hot gravel of the station yard, the sun warm on the down of peaches in boxes on the pavement, the hotel we chanced on.

After dinner we went out into the quiet, half-empty town and wandered about the streets.

We decided to stay for one or two days. We stayed the whole of our holiday—before its unexpected extension.

2

It was in Mirrepont that what had begun as almost the luxury of a personal reservation unimportant to anyone but me gradually became a sort of obstinacy, assumed the uncompromising nature of a moral conviction. I thought : nothing shall happen that isn't sought by her.

127

And later, the past less sharp, less significant than the present, doubts recreating themselves, it began to seem to me that perhaps I had been stupidly wrong, and she didn't mean, had never meant, never felt, anything but friendship—extreme, for she wasn't moderate, but only friendship. Or at any rate nothing involving sexual love. I thought perhaps it was true that so far as I was concerned she *was* now completely happy ; had all she wanted, or would want, to satisfy her.

That I shouldn't know whether this was so or not appeared to me absurd. But yet there was nothing in my experience for me to know, with any certainty, what could or couldn't be felt in an emotional context of fundamental normality.

We had been friends, I had neglected the friendship for other interests, and now we were friends again.

Was that, after all, a possibility ?

From Mirrepont we went to places and looked at things. I found that more and more as the days passed I was filling them with something to do.

Towards the end of our stay we went for the second time to the Lascaux caves.

We went with an English family who haa come to the hotel—people named Heath. He was a stockbroker. They had two children, a little girl about a year old, and a boy, and it was because Diana always talked to the children that we had become friendly with them. They were nice, pleasant to be with : if you could stand the continual reminder that it seemed you *could* have everything.

Diana didn't seem to mind it.

We started latish for the caves, and had to wait for the end of a French lunch-hour. From Montignac we had driven up the long hill to near where the entrance was, and she and I sat on the grass waiting. Mrs. Heath, having packed a special basket of things the baby would need for the day, had discovered that the basket had fallen off the luggage rack of their car, and she and her husband had gone off back to the village to see what they could buy there. Peter, the little boy, stayed with us.

He ran about playing with his kite.

She watched him, eating the remainder of a melon we had bought.

When she had finished, she got up and walked with the skin to where she could throw it out of sight into some trees. There were groups of people on the grass. She walked casually, consciously casual; self-conscious of her sex. She was wearing dark jeans and a summer jumper. The clothes echoed nakedly, tenderly, the body they covered : waist, breasts, her thighs. It was ordinary ; nothing special. One could have found in fewer minutes fifty girls dressed much the same. But the direct contact now with her pure charged physical attractiveness was intolerable to me ; like a torment.

I looked away.

Words came into my mind unwanted, Lawrence's words, used in conversation with Andrew. 'It's not the jeans and the jumpers, it's what they put in them.' Andrew had laughed.

Impersonality took over my own desire.

But then she came and sat where she had been sitting, touching me almost, and said something, wiping her

hands with her handkerchief, and she was Diana, not
' they ', and I wanted her, loving her.

" I'm sorry ; what did you say ? "

" Just, what were you thinking about ? "

" Nothing. That it's hot. Aren't you hot ? " She
blew out a puff of breath to agree that she was. " You'd
probably have been cooler in a dress."

" Darling, you're so right : after the event. I was
going to wear shorts but my legs want doing." Below
the jeans there was down just beginning on her legs.
" I meant to pack the stuff. Only meant to, though.
How do you pack and remember things ? Please lend
me some. I suppose you have a list."

" Typed out. In triplicate."

She laughed. " Of course. My system is thinking
what I'll need for everything. I start with my feet
and work up. I could hardly work down, could I ?
The system frequently goes to hell."

Peter called out to us, " Everyone look at me."

She paused to smile at him. " He's sweet, isn't he ?
Don't you think it's somehow touching he should look
so like his mother ? The faces are identical. He's a
very beautiful little boy." Then she said, " You know,
Mrs. Heath reminds me very faintly of my mother.
Not much, but just enough to remind me. I wonder if
you will think my mother is beautiful." She looked at
me. " I wonder what you will think of each other
when you meet ? "

" Shall we meet ? When shall we meet ? "

" Who knows ?—with my mother. Oh look, Judith,
how he's flying that kite. Like a ballet. He's showing

130

off. Did I tell you he asked me to go and see his boats?
He looks sweet in his bath. I made up sea shanties for
him."

Peter came up to us with his kite.

It was yellow, and practically as big as he was.

She smiled at him, and his kite, and was charming to
him.

Afterwards, when he had gone off again, I asked her
how many children she was going to have of her own.

"How many? You make it sound like a nursery."
But her voice was serious. "Two perhaps. Three.
If I'm rich. And happily married."

"Why wouldn't you be?"

"Happy? Well, everyone isn't. I was going to
say, you weren't. But *you* ought to have been. You're
the type. I'm not the kind of person to marry ; to make
a marriage last."

It was a marriage relationship I had thought of with
her ; in the sense that I had not thought of any time
when I would part from her. If I had somewhere
acknowledged that in the end it might be others keeping
her, for instance, from children, from the deepest fulfil-
ments of a feminine life, and not me, it was because I
knew the nature of the forces ranged against any perman-
ent sexual relationship between us—not because I feared,
as such, the kind of person she was.

The Heaths returned, and we walked together towards
the caves.

Mr. Heath wanted to know why we thought the
paintings had been done. "If it isn't all a joke, of
course."

His wife said she would so much rather it wasn't.

"If they weren't just artists," Diana said, "and wanted to paint them? Perhaps as a comfort, a kind of mental camp-fire. Or the usual so-called sublimation, I suppose."

Mr. Heath said, "Sexual sublimation?"

"Well, yes; if there really is such a thing." She laughed. "Not that there would probably have been much need. Didn't you just get on with it? Cudgel or be cudgelled? No complications. Much better, no doubt."

"I can't think I'd really have cared for either."

"Oh you," she said, looking at me. "Darling, you'd have contracted out of it all. You'd have taken refuge in some cave with a telephone and a boulder to sit behind. And sat lovingly letting leases. The Primitive Equitable."

"I have never let a lease."

"A maternal love. Properly watchful and possessive." She ruffled Peter's hair.

He was moderately interested in the paintings, as one might be in a side-show.

Going home, because he asked her to, Diana went in their car.

She gave no sign of being unwilling.

In consequence, Mr. Heath came with me. He chose his family to talk about; perhaps for my pleasure, but I think for his. Listening, I drove through the clear sunny evening.

Back at the hotel she said, "Did you like being with him? Did you talk about fortunes made and lost? Did he tell you he thinks you've gone brown better than any of us? Their maid said that as well. I love it when people say nice things about you."

She had changed, and come to my room. For the first time during the fortnight we had been away she was wearing a ring Andrew had given her before we came. (He had explained the gift with a good day in tin ; it had occurred to me since it was probably intended to compensate for Gerry.)

"Nice things about me, too," she added. "I've just met him on the landing. He said I looked like an Italian film star. I'd have said he was a bit short-sighted, only he seems very observant. He noticed Andrew's ring at once."

"Well, *observant* . . ."

The urge I had not so much to quarrel with her as oppose her mood of sociability and high spirits, the senseless urge, was detestable and overwhelming.

She laughed. "I was afraid it wasn't your cup of tea. It's why I haven't worn it. Still, one has to assert one's personality sometime, doesn't one ? "

"Of course."

"Is it far too big ? "

"I like it." That was true. I wouldn't have bought the ring, probably I wouldn't have bought a ruby. But I liked it ; especially on her.

"Nevertheless, you'd prefer it smaller ? "

"A little."

"Ken Heath thought the fun of it was being big. He thought it suited me. I knew he'd like it."

"After all, as a man, what he thinks is the more important."

133

In the silence that followed she stood looking at me. There was no way of telling what the look meant. Slowly, then, she took the ring off, and dropped it into a pocket of her dress.

I waited, saying nothing, doing nothing, unable, anyway, to free myself from the resolve that had assumed dictatorial powers.

When she spoke again, her voice was light and conversational : making a new start. "Did you know that where they're going in Paris has a chef who won a championship ? So Mrs. Heath says. For soufflés. She wants us to go and try one. I said we'd have dinner with them. Isn't it like her to have a passion for soufflés ? "

" I suppose it is."

" Why did you say it like that ? "

" Did I say it in any special way ? Heavens, don't analyse imaginary subtleties when all I'm doing is agreeing with you."

She turned away at this, and went from the room without speaking.

Later that evening, however, it was her suggestion that we should go to the cinema.

After a time in the uncommitted dark I picked up one of her hands, an act of conciliation, and began to play with the fingers. Though it had not been a part of what I intended, a stab of welcoming joy went through me as I did so. Life with its sets of situations, much alike, endlessly repeated : some for some people, some for others.

The joy didn't last.

A man sitting near us noticed what I had done. I

134

saw him looking at us afterwards as he smoked his cigarette in the disruptive French interval. His stare was inquisitive ; superficially interested, faintly pitying. I felt us utterly exposed to it.

Indifference would have been impossible. What would have helped, the only thing, I suppose, was a sense of absolute unity with her.

I experienced the familiar impulse : to go away from where I was, to escape into an existence where uncomforming desires were hidden, of no account, no test of one's value ; where in terms of work at least it was possible to go along with people, or settle differences from a position that was ordinary and equal. An existence behind Channing doors ; behind my office door, closed on emotional ' states ', on the thin, dull, sterile, infected, waiting worm of self-pity for one's state—on life as I couldn't live it.

Diana was gazing at pictures of film stars decorating the walls.

It was ironic the Frenchman should have seen us too soon.

On our last morning in Mirrepont we sat at a little table in the hotel garden, drinking coffee for breakfast. A hose lay on the dampened ground, which was already steaming. There were red and pink flowers in the garden ; the few dark roses smelt of pepper.

Paris was different.

We went to a cloudy Paris two or three days after the Heaths, on our way home. We looked at the convent where she had stayed ; we had dinner with Mr. and Mrs. Heath.

135

The restaurant was open to the city evening air—its windows opening on to streets vital and tense, it seemed to me, without being gay.

Mrs. Heath sat opposite her husband, warmed by her part in the evening as his wife.

A man with an accordion played a tune for her.

Looking away from her, away from Diana, out into the streets, I thought : though it's here the *closed* expressions of the French are most obvious, a Paris crowd can absorb anyone. Whoever goes by in it—I picked them out in turn as they went by—the beggar with a hairy face and dirty feet, the blue-haired woman clutching her young black, the hooded Holy Family of Nazareth sister, whoever goes by is safely a part of it.

And across the material of my thoughts, like a thin, bright thread that didn't match, came the thought that, if only she wanted to love me, we could go out into the crowd as lovers, Diana and I ; have our place in it, be uncaringly absorbed.

After dinner the two of us went up to the Sacré Cœur alone.

The taxi-driver who took us there and brought us back to our hotel was a young man, pleasant and talkative, who smoked a cigar. He was wittily erudite about his city. When I remember him I'm sorry he had such a poor audience ; at any rate so far as I was concerned.

He said good-night to us.

In the upright cupboard of the hotel's lift, a tiny secret world of chattery doors and glass and notices, we faced each other, very close.

136

She said, "To-morrow will be our last night." That was all she said; she didn't move.

No doubt it is a truism that the intelligence and the heart speak different languages, and of the two the intelligence is the less effectual; discovering it for oneself one must still surely be incredulous.

I was incredulous of all this; the continued childishness of it, my own childish failure to act one way or another. In fact, in the one way left to me.

I was incredulous.

But it did me no good.

I went to my room, and there imagined her with a husband, whose face was indefinite, a symbol, though it needn't have been, I knew it quite well; I imagined her having a tune played for her by a smiling accordionist.

I imagined loving her; as if it might happen.

The Heaths were staying another week. They had planned a picnic for the next day, and were going out of Paris by the same road that we were. They asked what time we were leaving, and said they would look out for us—to wave a final good-bye.

In the morning it seemed as if it would rain.

Diana said as we began to drive towards our port, "I thought about this the day we came. It felt so far away, and now suddenly we're doing it. I wonder if dying's like that."

Her attention was distracted by an old English taxi which had 'Charlie' on it in white paint, and was full of girls who were probably students; then all at once she exclaimed, "There are the Heaths. Look, in front!"

Mrs. Heath was driving.

137

" They've chanced the rain."

Accidents aren't climaxes, in the way—because of their violence and drama—one might imagine. One doesn't build up to them. They suddenly happen.

I remember Diana saying it was incredible to take chairs on a picnic, and that she would sit on the grass at a hundred. The Heaths hadn't noticed us. I was driving behind them and about to overtake when Mrs. Heath turned off left down a lane. If she gave any sign she was going to do this I didn't see it. I don't know how I didn't crash into them. I forced our car to the right, quite automatically, I don't remember doing anything, and waited for the crash : the noise, the deadly collapse of metal, the awfulness of savagery against human flesh.

I don't think anyone but I knew the brief second we missed that by, the splintered inch. Not Diana, even. I had a very indistinct impression of Peter suddenly waving as the Heaths went off out of sight down their lane.

I had stopped the car right up against the high kerb of the road, badly grating the wheels. Diana sat looking at me, surprised more than afraid ; in an innocence of the truth.

I can live the moment again by remembering it. The road seemed to have gone very quiet and still. A panel of morning light from between some trees cut across her face, and delved into the living, radiant skin, with its breathing pores, its life and warmth.

" Diana."

She smiled slightly, puzzled.

When I kissed her it wasn't as I had dreamt of it,

138

it was from shock and fear that turned into desperate thankfulness. I remember her cheekbone hard on my face. I don't know if she kissed me back. She didn't resist when I held her, as if safe in my embrace, until the fear began to dissolve.

"I love you. In all the ways I shouldn't; but I do love you."

3

We had driven back to Paris against the beginning of a pale grey rain barrier. The car was at a garage. Our only purpose now had become to talk.

There is a blankness about hotel bedrooms, the blankness of rooms that don't belong to anyone. She sat on the other side of the room in a small cushioned bedroom chair.

She said, " Had you stopped loving each other; you and Terry ? "

" It wasn't that. It was "—I paused, for putting into words just what it had been—" that everything about her except her senses believed women need men. Whether or not they want them or can have them."

" For prestige ? To be propped up socially ? "

" That's less trivial than you make it sound. Though what she was really afraid of was where going on with it would lead in a relationship like ours : two unprotected old maids. Unprotected and unproductive."

She frowned.

Held together, Terry had said, by the things that do hold people together : responsibility, loyalty, perhaps love—yet hating each other at heart for their final situation. Saying it, finding I had to say it despite the part of me in open revolt against further reservation, objection, scruple, now what had happened had happened —had to say it because the life Diana would live continued inescapably and *really* to matter, if anything mattered, if human beings mattered—I had a sudden consciousness of brutality. " Women don't stop being women because they love women."

" And if it couldn't have been different ? The babies —and everything. If it couldn't have been different ? "

" Doesn't one always think it could have been different ? "

A Velocette darted noisily by outside in the rain.

" Judith—was Terry why you married Martin ? "

" I married him after her."

" I could never talk much to you about Martin. It wasn't what you said, but you looked as if you minded. Marrying Martin didn't work for you ; did it ? " There was a pause. Then, " Was she like me ? " she asked.

" No. Not really like you."

" Often people go on falling in love with the same type, I think. In the way they keep writing the same book. Not that it was why I asked. Did you love her more than me ? "

" No. I loved her."

" Italians are passionate. What was she like ? "

" Does it matter ? Do you really want to know ? She came from Naples. She was very—*un*tragic. And

140

she was sure that in the end we should be tragic. That was really her whole point : that you mustn't go on long enough for that. I saw the point ; but I am better at falling in love than out of it."

"People can always be miserable in the end. Gerry's mother and father are. And that Belgian woman in the train," she added suddenly ; "you remember. She was as miserable as anyone I've seen, and she had a rich and doting husband—once."

"She had a reasonable chance. She didn't start off against the tide. It's a very strong tide. Leaving aside any question of babies, of things like that ; of still being a woman. As a homosexual man I could have been in prison. As a woman I would automatically be thought depraved. And unsavoury." For the first time she glanced away. The inward compulsion, not choice, certainly not choice, made me go on, "It's what most people feel. What they feel is terrifying. And it isn't even only that. It's—oh, all the books you ever read being wrong, all the plays you see, the talk you listen to. The whole of life the wrong way round."

She didn't look at me. Dark ends of hair curved in against her neck. I noticed the faint lines of vein running, bruise-like, upwards from her wrist.

"Diana, listen. I have nothing to lose ; but if you have the least chance of doing without me, or someone like me, of arranging your life differently, take it. Don't start with me unless you must. Don't believe we shall live happily ever after."

"I don't want an affair with you," she said. She was facing me again. "Being just something that

141

happened once. I couldn't, now. I don't want kissing you in cars and saying good-bye."

" That would be easier."

" People don't love because it's easier ; or because they think they'll be happy, even. It isn't like that."

" What is it like ? " I heard my tone become gentler.

" What was it like, for me ? " She picked up a new packet of cigarettes, slit the cellophane ; thinking. " Shall I try to tell you ? It's hard, but I'll try and tell you. At first, you see, I was just interested, terribly interested—in everything to do with you. You had a kind of glamour. Then I started getting emotional about you. I didn't know why, but it was the first time, and I didn't much care. It was the first time." She gave a brief, barely voiced laugh. " And it was something so terribly important to life. I hadn't believed it would happen to me, not like this, but it had. Everything in my life began being related to you. And everything about you mattered. What you said, whether you were happier sometimes than others ; what you felt about me." She paused. " I didn't know really what you felt about me."

I was silent.

" I knew I had to see you, be with you. I began to know I needed you. As well as everything else, the kind of stillness and certainty in you."

" *Certainty ?* Oh, darling."

" And I'd felt at first," she went on, " there was something about you I almost had to stand up to ; overcome. Something, oh, I can't exactly explain, the way you didn't behave intimately with people, a sort of coolness

142

in the way you behaved. Then, when there wasn't that, when you didn't do it with me, it was—oh, well." The last words she had spoken softly. " I loved being near you. I loved touching you, and if you touched me. I didn't think of any more than that. I didn't think of loving you, of making love. Not until that evening at your flat when you kissed my hair. Then I wanted us to be in love, terribly."

I was looking at her.

" I knew what it meant. Of course. That it wasn't normal. Perhaps I didn't know quite all of what it meant. Or quite think of it then as being for always. But I didn't care what it was. I was just terribly happy that you loved me." She stopped. " Only afterwards," she said, " I was sure you'd thought better of it, whatever you felt. Because you weren't the type. I thought it was why we never talked about it. Behaved as though nothing had happened."

" The type ? "

" You see, I thought you'd decided not to involve yourself. That for you it was too beyond the pale. Which was why you'd lit the blue touchpaper and retired immediately."

I said at last, " So would you have just, well—let it go ? "

With a sudden sharp movement she stripped the cellophane from the cigarettes. " I was afraid if I tried to do what you didn't want I might lose you. Altogether. I'd have accepted anything rather than that. I'd have accepted just what you decided we were to have. No love-making, then no love-making. Nothing had ever

143

happened, anyway, to make me think sex was everything. Happiness for me with you wasn't going through all the motions. Then." She crumpled up the paper in her hand. " Besides, I didn't want to be a nuisance to you any more."

" Could it really have been like that ? " I stood gazing at her. Finally I added, " But it was *only* that ? "

" Though it was hard all the same to think of us as anything so classified as homosexuals." She had just hesitated before the term.

" It doesn't come easily."

" Even this morning."

" I didn't mean this morning to happen."

" It was that none of it seemed to have anything to do with you ; nothing that I knew, or had imagined. I'd heard it talked about ; and had people pointed out to me once or twice. I remember Vic did. Queers, he called them. Funny : we could have what men like that'll ruin their lives for, and they could have either of us with shoes and rice. I'd read things in books, of course, something in a French girl's novel once about some horrible club where a lot of women in leather jerkins danced with a lot of other women and everyone was more or less drunk on gin. There was something in a war book I read, too, about sinister sisterhoods, and obscenity. And I know prostitutes are often lesbians. And everyone's heard of touting at tubes. But none of it had anything to do with us ; with you."

" I couldn't tell you anything about the clubs if you wanted me to. I suppose they exist. I haven't got a

144

leather jerkin. And when I go into a tube it's to get somewhere ; because it's less trouble than the car. There are other things I can't help having to do with. The things Terry believed women must have."

" What would I have without you ? "

" Everything ?—in the end ? "

Her look now didn't move from my face. "I love you. You haven't only given me being loved, you've given me loving."

There was a silence which felt very long. She didn't break it, but came slowly over to where I stood. She was frowning slightly. Without coquetry she kissed my mouth.

4

Doesn't it seem to be rather generally believed that women in their sexual relations want to be dominated ? At any rate it is a convention of thought. I didn't want to be dominated, nor did I want to dominate. There was no suggestion when we made love of the pretended masculine partner, the woman one imagines lean and mannish ; we gave and we took, both of us, equally.

I hadn't known how it would be for her. There was Gerry, after all—it was with him she perhaps could have begun a taste of the senses, whether or not she was aware of it. At first I wanted above all to be emotionally sensitive to her ; and adroit.

Then this became the concern with oneself of ordinary

145

passion : melting into pleasure and the tenderness which comes from pleasure, and into gratitude.

In a successful novel about love, written with the specialist's air of knowledge, I had read once that even the most sensible of women are subconsciously rather afraid to be despised after they have let themselves be made love to. What is claimed for the subconscious is hard to deny. But if, in reverse, it is possible to feel contempt for such a reason, I am astonished.

We had gone to the impersonal bed, with its coolness and blankness. I could feel her still trembling. Her slip was white, with lace where it contained her breasts. The lace and the nylon were very white ; with an odd digression of the mind at a time when one hardly thinks I remembered something she had said, amused, about being told at school that what one wore under one's dress was of greater importance than the dress.

She said, " 'At last, at last, or some such rot.' " The words broke in the middle, as if she had swallowed because her mouth was dry.

I knew I had read the words somewhere or heard them, perhaps in a film, but I didn't know where, or try to place them.

" Judith."

" Oh, darling."

I think her passion surprised me ; it had in it a quality of *gladness*, I think it was, that a little surprised me.

The afternoon darkened, and the rain with it.

She almost slept.

It was her idea that we should go back to Mirrepont.

146

" On the spur of the moment and leaving everything behind ? "

She remembered, and half smiled. " Only this time," she said, " it will be what it was supposed to be."

We went back to make love in the sun.

5

Everything hinged on the man who stood in the road as we approached him from Uzerche going towards Mirre-pont and waved at us to stop. I probably wouldn't have stopped if I had thought about it ; the road was lonely. But I braked automatically when I saw him.

He was standing by a motor-bike which had a box with tools in it instead of a side-car. That we were foreigners rather took him aback, and he explained through the window of the car with an uneasy mixture of brusqueness and embarrassment that what he wanted was petrol—just enough to get him to a garage.

I told him I hadn't any. Except in the tank.

He then explained that he had a tube he could use to get petrol from our tank to his.

When I had backed the car so that it was alongside his bike, Diana got out to watch. I heard her talking to him as he searched for his piece of tube. To begin with he merely answered her ; but gradually his politeness became less gruff. He asked her where we were going, and said something or other about his sister. Most of it, however, I could barely hear and

147

didn't follow. I knew he said his sister was a widow. ' *Veuve* '.

Afterwards he offered me two hundred francs.

When I refused it, he thanked me with a small movement which could almost have been a bow, and went back to his bike. He stood waving to us as we drove off.

Diana said, " His sister has a little hotel on the road to Souillac ; after you get to Mirrepont. He comes from Souillac. He was quite poetic about it. I suppose he was trying to do some business for her. . . ."

The small sunny garden, she assured me when we arrived there, the steps in rock leading up from the road to the restaurant, were just as he had said.

The restaurant was small ; it had chequered tablecloths and frilly, frivolous curtains, and was full of flowers. There was a smell of hot butter and garlic. Brass and bottles were doubled in dark wood which had been polished everywhere until it had a sultry glow.

When we first arrived, new there, with nothing to explain, two women were in the garden. They were both immensely fat. One was in black, a very old lady sitting on a box in the shade, her back against a waterbutt. She was trying to read a newspaper. The other, who was younger, the sister we had heard about, was doing some washing as she talked. She seemed to have a natural talkativeness.

Seeing the car, she came towards us and greeted us with phrases and gestures that amounted to elegance. Her feet bulged out of a pair of plimsolls, and the apron tied round her waist appeared to have been threaded through her.

148

She chatted all the time as she showed us our room. Afterwards she made us sit in the garden, and going down into her stone cellar returned with a bottle of Monbazillac and two bottles of mineral water. She wrote the number of our room on the Monbazillac. " *Voilà, mesdames !* " she said.

A little later she was back with two or three postcards of the hotel, which she handed to us, smiling.

Something of the place's extraordinary charm had been caught on the postcards. I sent one of them to Helen, explaining that I should be in France longer than I had planned. Later I learnt that she kept it, and used it for making conversation. To Julian, at any rate.

Our first days with Madame Chabal were enchanted ; charged with a central bliss that lit all the warm pleasures we had returned to. That I cannot convey with words my happiness at that time seems not to be important. The experience is too common to need clarifying with words. Our love in essence was like million upon million of love affairs. It was made up of such things as finding her sleepily beside me in the morning, of waking in the night to find she was awake, too ; her extravagant endearments when she wasn't serious, her speaking of my name when she was. It had the hot sun and the French countryside as a part of it. And the river, now.

Afternoon after afternoon we spent in the riverside hut Madame Chabal had let to us. Her husband had used it for fishing.

We talked there ; swam, and got dry again in the sun ; made love ; played records on a gramophone belonging to her son.

The son was in Japan, and had a collection of records, some Bach among them, and a lot of Rachmaninoff—Diana loved the Rachmaninoff, and played the Third Piano Concerto until I almost grew tired of it—his mother doubted if he would return to play again.

I read a good deal.

Our new relationship, for me, had much in it of an emancipation. I could at times now effortlessly go my own way, and read, or just lie looking at the green river verge and the smooth, clear surface of the water, thinking of anything, of things quite remote from her. I no longer had any feelings about couples in dark doorways. With so much else she had given me a balance, a new freedom. A new tranquillity.

I began even not to ask myself if the relationship between us rested on, was the result of, no more than just an accident : or whether somehow, in some fashion, the kiss would have been chosen, would have happened, anyway. It was past. It was theoretic.

And she seemed so happy.

She wrote a poem. She said it was for the first time. She didn't keep it, and she wouldn't give it to me. She just said that it wasn't very good ; and that 'lake' was poetic licence, 'river' wouldn't have fitted—but that she had wanted to write a poem. However, I almost remember it still. I remember it began :

> ' Out of creation for the heart's song,
> For the mindless moment of delight :
> A lake's blue silence,
> And the wakeful night
> Lain in the burnished bowl of the land.'

150

A brush of high trees in the sun, climbing; petals, golden wings, on a hot hill; slanted summer rain, singing. I think those were the other things she chose.

It ended :

> ' But of all things, still,
> Most destined to this joy
> None
> More than the flesh of my love
> In her summertime,
> The warm flesh, and the blood's call.'

The poem meant something fundamental to me.

But she laughed at herself as a poet. " If I'm going to be anything," she said, " it'll have to be a novelist. It was just that I never believed it could be like this ; that's all."

Soon afterwards she took to getting up early, and writing at the window of our bedroom—slacked and sweatered, her feet on the ledge, reminding me in those moments of a model in some teen-agers' magazine.

The first time it happened I woke up, vaguely aware of being looked at. " The reason," she said, " you take up too much of the bed, I have just discovered, is that you sleep with your head on the edge of it, lulled by a misplaced sense of virtue, while the rest of you sort of arcs itself out."

" What are you doing ? "

" It's all right. I am. I really am. I'm doing some work." She paused. " You know, I've never thought much of writing as a sublimation ; it seems a bit irrelevant.

151

But making yourself work and letting yourself love : that's the perfect arrangement."

Her eyes looked quite tired from writing.

It was a moment when I loved her very much.

The next day she came to me.

" U.S.," she said.

" What is ' U.S.' ? "

" It's Airforce. Or it was. My father said it. It means unserviceable."

"Don't *you* say it. Anyhow, it isn't true."

" From to-morrow I will cease to have been born vulgar." Suddenly she laughed. " You're a romantic, of course."

"Do you think so?" I kissed her.

About a week after this we went to the hut for an entire day. We told Madame Chabal in the morning, and she packed us a picnic lunch, saying she would expect us back to dinner—as early or as late as we liked. She told us mind the sun.

By afternoon the heat had a quality of clinging velvet gold, and I lay in the doorway of the hut, half mesmerised, transfixed by a sensuous laziness ; unwilling even to swim. Diana was still in the water.

There were two or three other people bathing, and she had been chatting with a thickly-built, brown Frenchman who sat on the bank most of the time, his back glistening, only his feet in the water, watching her.

When she was ready to come out, he bent down and, taking her under the arms, lifted her on to the grass. He released her at once. She smiled at him—then ran towards the hut.

152

It wasn't doubt that I felt, or jealousy; just the tremor of a desire to be reassured.

Momentarily she stood in the sun. "Do you know," she said, "I've been out of cigarettes since last night. I suppose I could go and get some. I suppose I could give up. I'll give up." She laughed, and touched my face as she went into the hut. "What more do I need? I'm going to get dressed now. Darling, mind your legs."

She pushed the door to.

"Diana."

She was kneeling on the sun-warm boards, drying herself. She looked up.

"Oh," she said. "Not getting dressed."

"Come here."

She came to me.

I pulled her down by my side, and kissed her hair, and throat, and mouth. "It's what I wanted to do that Sunday."

"You should have done."

"And you will always say that?"

"Yes," she said, her willing nakedness against mine. I could just hear the "yes," for already her mouth with concentration was tracing, in turn, the outline of my breasts.

As I began to caress her, a sweet sense of possession grew in me.

I do not know why, when I am a woman, a woman's body should hold such magic for me. Hers was smooth, and so soft one could be cradled in it, lost; yet it was beautifully contained within its own design.

Suddenly, a small sound, she caught her breath. But

153

I disregarded it, persisting in what it was that I wanted, the feeling, I suppose, that she was utterly, unreservedly, and only mine.

Though the small sound was repeated, she tightened her embrace. "My love, my love," she said.

We lay, intent on the passion and pleasure of expressing our love.

If it sounds immoral, offensive, whatever word, it didn't seem these things; it seemed natural. That is the contradiction: to see as perverse what one feels to be natural. Never could passion have felt more natural, more innocent than it felt to me with her. It felt innocent and luminous from loving each other.

A small cylinder of sunlight came through the doors.

6

"Do you want a cigarette?"

"No. I don't want anything."

We heard the Frenchman pass by, talking to a girl in his entreating, interior French voice.

"Off with the new, on with the old. Oh, well," she said.

"If it isn't one thing, it's another."

"Not really. Really, everything is heaven. Judith." She turned towards me. "What are we going to do when we get home? I mean——"

"I know what you mean. Do you want to come and stay at the flat? What would you say to Andrew?"

"I've no idea. That London is where a writer should live? Perhaps it is. Do you promise about living with you?"

"It is a silly thing to promise."

When we spoke again it was because she had made a move to get up. I put out my hand to stop her.

"Darling, I was going to let in a bit more air. Though I dare say it's more your rôle than mine at heart. The human species can be divided temperamentally into two distinct groups—fresh-air-o-philes and draught-o-phobes."

"In a minute. In just a minute."

She laughed, and came back into my arms.

Not more than a moment or two after that, the doors were pushed open and Julian stood looking at us.

He said, no longer concerned with speech, "I'm

155

sorry, I didn't really think you were here, that anyone was in here, I——"

Sun flowed over the hut. Momentarily he continued
to look at us, motionless. He had on a light grey suit ;
his hair appeared almost blond from the sun.

The moment was irreclaimable ; its truth self-evident.
There was nothing that could be done for it. Only one
thing could have made it worse—that anyone should try.

Conscious of Diana without realising that I had looked
at her, I saw the skin under one of her eyes quiver slightly,
seem to recoil ; that was all. After she had sat up,
she didn't move or speak.

" I'm sorry," Julian said again, this time in possession
of himself, his face now expressionless. And he turned
and left the hut.

That such occurrences, by their very nature, border
on farce, I do not doubt. *Flagrante delicto.* This was
not the aspect of it which struck me.

I could still see him in my mind as he walked away
over the quiet, giving grass.

7

" Madame Chabal must have told him we were here.
What will he do ? "

" I don't know what there is he can do : that he
would."

" Oh heavens, why did he have to choose exactly
then ? "

156

"'Then' could have been so often; couldn't it? I didn't even think of——"

"Anyway, it isn't his business." She seemed suddenly to decide on the line she would take; perhaps brace herself with it. "People's love affairs aren't anyone else's business. Nobody outside them. Besides: let him think of the primeval bang or continuous creation; then he'll want something to worry about, worrying about us."

"His conception of either would probably only convince him more we were to be *worried* about."

She looked at me. "You aren't going to let it make any difference?"

"Not if you don't want me to."

"We don't belong to anyone else. We haven't even anything to give worth giving: except to each other. We're free to do as we like."

She frowned at my silence.

I said, "I wonder if we are. Overtly. To do it blatantly."

"So what do you suggest?" Something indistinguishable from anger had come hurriedly into her voice. "Do you mean you don't want me to live with you at the flat? Is it to be kissing in cars, after all? Just secret, furtive kissing in cars? Creeping furtively about in the dark. Are we just going to give up what matters most, being together, really being together, as an act of—good taste?" Her face expressed her opinion of this. Then she said, the anger all at once quite gone, her voice quite quiet, "It isn't blatant not to be blackmailed by other people's attitude to something you aren't ashamed of yourself."

157

8

We had managed to get an air passage home. Driving to the airport we stopped next to a Scotsman involved in the same traffic jam that we were ; he leant across from his window as we all waited to move on a farther few inches, and asked, to encourage us, " Everything all right ? "

Diana said, yes.

I had tried to imagine being Julian ; not just to imagine being myself more or less in his place. I knew that though discovering he was a homosexual would have surprised me, and only surprised me—since where there is no feeling of sin there is no moral affront—this was scarcely relevant. What I didn't know was that it would have been sounder to imagine discovering him a sadist, a child murderer : something that would have aroused in me not only natural revulsion but the desire to act. As it was, though the thought of having to see him again now hung wretchedly over the present and the future, I wasn't in any real sense of the word alarmed.

However, after we had been home some time I still hadn't seen him ; still didn't know—which was what I had asked myself—whether he would want to end his personal relations with me, completely. He had gone to Northern Ireland from France. Not that I had heard this from him. Andrew told me at the August board meeting.

It was the kind of meeting that, because of one person, feels pressed for time. Rivers had had some difficulty

158

over a bank loan for one of his other companies, and he was anxious to return his attention to it as quickly as possible.

"Give you an umbrella on a fine day, and the first wet day they want it back again," he said.

The atmosphere wasn't helpful to Betty Shaw and her mortgage.

Betty had told me since I'd been back from France that she and Tom wanted to get married. They'd found a house they wanted to buy. It was very small and it wasn't very nice. But they wanted it for a home. Not that strictly speaking they had the money to buy anything. Tom had been true to reputation as a sailor.

"Young people should save," observed Rivers.

Lawrence said, " Ah well, we'll be doing the chap a favour if we turn it down. There's always the park. Girls might be a dead loss if they aren't interested, but my God they're a dead weight when they are ! Love and marriage till it makes you sick."

All the same, he could have married a girl to-morrow, publicly, applauded and approved of.

I said, " Perhaps they don't want the park. They want to get married. Perhaps what they want is living together. Reading the paper at breakfast, and knowing there isn't any hurry at night. Things like that. Not just some sort of homeless association."

He looked surprised.

Immediately I regretted my words—which, after all, apart from being somewhat earnest (it wasn't a subject to encourage much light-heartedness in me) were to do with my business, and not the afternoon's.

159

" Well, I wasn't serious," he said.

" We can't always have what we want," said Rivers.

" Only what we can afford." Andrew polished briefly at a cuff-link. Gold ; like the tooth when he smiled. " Or what other people afford us." Then to me he remarked, with abrupt friendliness, " My dear Judith, as from time to time I have to remind you, the Channing may be a service but it isn't a charitable institution. Still, I suppose you might call the girl a valued employee. In these days. It must be all of eighteen months we've enjoyed her typing. Even allowing for the number of times she's been late. Perhaps we ought to find her a hundred or two."

Nobody seriously argued.

All the men there were capable on occasion of being immovable over something that was purely business. But when it was a matter of the personal element, a definite lead would as a rule quite easily sway them, particularly if it didn't come from me. As a woman I was assumed to need watching in case anything got the better of my head.

" Well, we've spent enough time on Miss Shaw," said Rivers at the first opportunity. " Probably we should have spent less if she had been less personable. So we're to do what we can for them. Mr. Ellis, these forms——"

" Yes, Mr. Rivers. Where do you suggest we——? "

" It would seem as well to begin with the first and work rapidly upwards."

By the time the meeting was over Betty Shaw had been forgotten, but Andrew said to me that I had sounded

160

very domestic. "Is there some Frenchman in the story we haven't heard about?"

"I haven't heard about him either."

"Did my niece cut you out?"

"I was obliterated."

"At any rate Floyd will be relieved."

It was at this that I asked him if he had heard from Julian; whether he was still in France.

"Are you trying to find out what I know? Or is it possible you don't? He's gone to see his parents. I gather his old father isn't any too well."

I took in the information without comment.

Then, just before we parted, he said—and his voice had altered, he seemed to be making something of an effort—"I miss her but I've been meaning to say it's kind of you, having Diana to stay at your flat. I never imagined living with me was exactly ideal for her. Still, there was no home at all when my sister went off." He paused. "I suppose a girl that age needs a woman, to give an eye to things; a girl of her sort. And Paley's been no bloody good to her. Self-centred young bastard. All as obvious to you, no doubt, as to me. Well, anyway, Judith, many thanks for what you're doing."

I left him as quickly as I decently could to go into my own office—where I worked hard until later than usual.

Diana was waiting for me, outside in the street. The new caretaker had got the car, and she came up to it as I was getting in.

She said, "I was afraid I'd missed you."

"What are you doing out here?" I opened the door wider for her.

"It was only you I wanted to see."

"Is anything the matter?"

"No."

She smiled.

I was sharply conscious of her in the small prison of the car as I started the engine : her aware face, her hands, lying one on the other in her lap. It was like having one's senses switched on ; having a vital part of one all at once warmly functioning. With my moment of imprecise anxiety dispersed by the smile, I found myself, in spite of what had been said earlier, alive with pleasure at her sudden, unexpected nearness.

"It's always strange when people call you 'Mrs. Allart '," she said. "It was, when he did. Phillips, isn't his name? Whatever I think of you as it's never Mrs. Allart. Gerry says he calls you Judith and thinks of you as Mrs. Allart."

"I never think of him as 'Mr. Paley '. When did he say that?"

We stopped-and-started our way through the London traffic.

"Oh, ages ago. But as it happens he called this afternoon. It made me think of him. He had the day off."

Gerry was now in the laboratory at a subsidiary company of his father's near Reigate.

"I told him I was working," she said, "which I was— but it didn't do much good. That's why I said I had to go out." She drew a rapid circle with her finger on the dashboard. "It's a bit awkward about Gerry. He can't understand why it's quite different now, and

162

I don't know what to tell him. He thinks it's because of Andrew. I can't say I don't love him any more because he never supposed that I actually did—only that I might."

"You could say that you *do* love someone else."

"For him to ask who? He's not like you are. He'd insist on an answer. Oh well," she said, "never mind," changing the subject : "it's an exciting evening. It's an exciting, heavenly evening ; have you noticed? You are the only person in the world I would want to be going home with."

London was generating a dry, August evening glow. Streets and trees which all day had seemed hot and lifeless now seemed electric.

"We *are* going home? " she added.

"Yes, darling ; wherever you like."

But all the same to go home was what I would have chosen, too. So far as I was concerned now, home, hers and mine, besides being the centre of our relationship, had become somewhere to retreat from personal relations with anyone else—which I had found myself wanting repeatedly to do since what had happened with Julian in France. I suppose it was like the idea of a South Sea island when the world seems to have little to offer but conflict. At any rate, when I wasn't working now, if I wasn't at home with her I thought of it with longing.

She called to me from the kitchen, " I'm glad we bought the black cups ; though they make me want a Mercedes Benz to go with them. Not that I've seen one, as far as I know, but the name's all style and shine."

"When they make films of your books you will be able to have a Harlequin set."

"Of Mercedes Benz? Yes. A plural, a plural, my kingdom for a plural. No, not this kingdom for any number of plurals. Not for anything. We. *We* will have the Harlequin set."

I was getting changed in the bedroom.

She came in, still with—unthinkingly—one of the cups in her hand. She laughed, and put it down on the radio by the bed. "It's a pretty little radio. The first time we went out you said, 'I'm not in the least tired. When I get home I shall put on the radio and listen to some jazz.' Do you remember?" Already, I thought, this bond of 'do you remember?' "And now it's both of us."

I nodded.

The black tea-cup, half dried and stood on the radio, seemed momentarily a symbol of ordinariness; of domestic stability.

She had taken off her stockings and girdle to put on slacks, and left them lying in my room. I made of these a symbol of emotional and domestic stability.

Then she said, "I'm glad at any rate Julian Floyd isn't the type to go starting trouble. I'm glad you're sure he isn't. Though he doesn't seem exactly in a hurry to seek us out. I couldn't bear everything to be upset. All this. I love you too much. Does it really just go on and on? Loving you so much. I would never have believed it of myself. Isn't the cure really a cure at all?"

"Cure?" I looked at her.

She kissed me as she gave me my blouse. "'. . .
No cure for love," she said, "neither meat nor drink

164

nor any charm, but only——' " She stopped. " It's
Daphnis and Chloë. Did you know? But every time
I'm ' cured ' makes me want you more, because you are
more familiar, more precious, because you seem more a
part of my deepest being. Every time we ' kiss, embrace,
lie side by side '."

" You are very sweet."

" I am very happy."

" In spite of all the things that should be different ? "

" Since it's you I love," she said, " nothing should be
different. Except that I needn't be thought lost ; not
for this. So that I can't tell Gerry, even. Except
that you wouldn't have to mind either. Not if everyone
knew."

" How much would you mind? If everyone did."

I was unprepared for quite the possessiveness I felt
towards her as I asked the question. I suppose I needn't
have been. There is no deliberate setting of a limit, any
limit, on feelings of love, whatever one's intention—
and if it hadn't always been so, consciously acknowledged,
my whole intention now for our future was that we should
share our lives, as well as a home. Just what happiness
this would bring, or misery, I didn't know any better
than I had ever known it ; but I could no longer think
of a different future. It had become, quite simply,
vital to me that we should stay together, that she should
feel as I felt. Though I believed she did, my situation,
inevitably, was wide open to the intrusion of doubts.

" I don't see how anyone could *not* hate it," she
said. " Do you? Think who ' everyone ' would be !
But——"

The phone went.

With reluctance, I answered it.

Martin said, surprisingly, "It isn't very convenient, is it? Are you washing your hair? Or have you a gamekeeper under the bed? I won't come, anyway. I'll come another time."

He rang off.

It was several days before he telephoned again, to ask if I was free the following Saturday. "Or when are you free?" he said. "I still haven't heard about your holiday. And there's something I want to show you, before the weather breaks. It will make you laugh."

I said I was free on Saturday. It had appalled me that his invitation, his, should have seemed no more than an irrelevance : not wanted, not welcome. And, anyway, I *was* free.

The day turned out to be hot and cloudy. He drove us to some field over the edge of Surrey into Hampshire, and there was what he wanted to show me.

It was a gypsy caravan, red and yellow, with curly wood, and a tin chimney.

I had never been inside a true caravan before. The cut glass trilled and turned extravagantly. The range, in contrast, was businesslike and small.

From the window one could see more fields and a stream.

"A pastoral setting," Martin said. "I got the caravan for a hundred, though they were asking a hundred and twenty. Last month, when it was raining ; and you were browning yourself under southern skies."

"Well, fairly southern."

He invited me to sit down on one of the bench-like

166

wooden seats, and sat opposite me. " Did you get as far as St. Flour ? By any chance."

" St. Flour. St. Flour. No, that wouldn't really have been on our road."

" I had a picture postcard a student of mine sent me from there of a black Christ. She said it was pretty marvellous. Very moving. If wood turns black, of course, it can add wonderfully to the effect."

" The best carvings I saw were at Albi. Or the ones I liked most. We had a day there from Mirrepont. They were wonderful. But, heavens, it was a drive by the time we'd finished ! We were practically sleep-walking at the end of that day."

" I've read about Albi. Choir boys and voluptuous maidens. Which reminds me : how is Diana ? "

" Very well."

" What are the new arrangements in aid of ? Have you embarked on some sort of foster-mothering ? "

" Not that, exactly."

" Well, you would hardly put it like that, I suppose." He half smiled. " But, anyway, I should think she can quite do with it, whatever it is. If you feel like the job. She gives the impression of being a bit motherless : not to say sisterless and brotherless."

" ' Four Winds ' is rather a long way from London for her."

" And Andrew a long way from filling the bill. No doubt you are much more what is needed."

I couldn't bring myself to answer this.

" Do you know, it's four o'clock," he said. " And going to *pour*. Shall we have some tea ? "

The thunder started when we were having tea, and worked itself up into a storm. I dislike bad storms, and at the height of this one was glad to reinforce myself with his unmoved male presence. He sat with the caravan door open, talking, smoking, watching the lightning as it struck at the surrounding fields. The fact that he was wearing old flannel trousers and a sports jacket with leather round the cuffs and at the elbows was obscurely reassuring. His tie was new, a very bright yellow. Only when gales of rain forced him to it did he close the door.

It was towards the end of the storm, as he was opening it again an hour or so later, that I noticed a hair-grip on the ledge by the bunk-like bed.

The significance of this, so far as it affected me, was not that he came to his caravan with girls, a girl—I didn't know or mind—but that, though he did do it, he should still want to come with me. And momentarily, as if in passing, I felt once more something that was like guilt, something acknowledging that to hand back someone's freedom doesn't have to be enough ; doesn't have to be any reparation at all.

Perhaps caught, as happens, on the point of what had passed through my mind, he laughed as he returned to sit down, this time next to me, and said, " It's ironic, isn't it, this situation should have occurred with you ? Marooned in a desert caravan."

But already I was thinking again of Diana : that I had to meet her and wouldn't be there.

She had been asked to have dinner with somebody from Elstree. Probably it is routine for film companies

168

to invest dinners in new writers. Anyway, she was being taken to the Café Royal, and we had arranged to meet afterwards in a bar she knew near Piccadilly.

The roads going home were greasy and difficult.

" I'm afraid you're going to be too late, anyway," Martin said. " Do you remember who lives near here ? "

I glanced at him.

He mentioned the name of a couple who had been friends of ours when we were married.

The wife had finally had a baby after about ten years. I recalled them mostly, now, for the occasion two or three years ago when the husband, Peter, had shocked my aunt to the point of her refusing to see them again by saying that he was living on steak and Joyce had taken to riding a bicycle but that they might have to fall back on a fountain-pen in the end.

" Shall we knock on the door and congratulate Joyce ? " Martin said. " I had a card from them. It's a boy."

" Diana——"

" You could phone."

" I'm not really sure of the name of the place ; and I only know the Christian name of the man who runs it. I——"

" All right," he said. " Are you jealous of Joyce ? "

" Jealous ?   No."

" You wouldn't like to have had a child ? "

" There must be very few women without one who wouldn't like to have had a child.   But nobody has everything ; after all."

" That is a very ordinary thing to have had."

" I'm not jealous, all the same."

I was more than an hour late, and she wasn't in Zgymunt's. However, as I was turning to go, somebody I knew came up to me from one of the stools at the bar ; somebody tall, with an eager face, and reddish hair, and restless, young man's body.

"Mrs. Allart," he said. "Judith."

"Gerry."

We looked at each other. "Gerry, where's Diana ? Do you know ? Are you with her ? "

"She's gone back to your flat to see if you were there." Then he insisted on buying me a drink before explaining the rest of what had happened. He didn't have anything more himself.

"Well, this is half the original plan at any rate," he said as he came back with my drink from the bar, and sat down. It was characteristic of him to sit rather on the edge of chairs, as if he was about to do something else ; as if he hadn't much time for sitting. "Diana let it drop she was meeting you here, and I didn't imagine I'd be gate-crashing anything, only you two girls, so I thought I'd just turn up and pay for the drinks."

"Oh, I see."

"Life's short," he added, "and I can't say I've been exactly seeing too much of her lately." He made a face. "But you weren't here, and the film chap was still tagging along. He put her in a taxi. Generally I was a bit of a crowd."

I drank some of my sherry.

"Anyway, I thought I'd hang on and see if you came. At least I could tell you what had happened."

"That was nice of you."

170

He smiled. " As a matter of fact, there was something else, too. I wanted to see you. About Diana."

" About Diana ? What about her ? "

" Could you tell me if it's just because of Andrew she's cold-shouldering me ? Or if there's anything else." He waited, his gaze direct.

" Is she cold-shouldering you ? " I said, trying to buy time, not ready for the question, and immediately uneasy at its nature.

" She's certainly not the same as she was. Actually I looked in on Andrew last night," he continued. " I was going to see if I could sort things out a bit. But I didn't get the chance. He couldn't wait to tell me again I'm not the kind of chap he wants hanging round his niece. He's living in another age, I think. So that was that. Things ended up worse than before, if possible. We can't hit it off. And if that's the way he feels, he'll just have to get on with it so far as I'm concerned. I don't know how much he's been on at Diana, though. Or—— Look, is there anyone else, do you know ? "

" I—— "

" If there's someone else she's in love with, well, all right. But I don't think it is that. I mean, it doesn't seem like it. Still, you'd know. She's pretty friendly with you now, isn't she ? "

" She's working very hard," I said. " She wants to finish her novel as soon as she can."

" I know. But all work makes Diana a dull girl, and that's not like her, you must admit. Has she *said* anything to you about it ? "

At a loss, I shook my head.

171

" Still, I suppose you know her pretty well by now. Even if she hasn't said much. Mrs. Allart, is there anything you think I ought to do about getting on the right side of her again? It's no good beating your head against a brick wall. But is there anything I'm doing wrong? If it isn't Andrew."

" I don't think it's Andrew. Anyway, she likes you very much."

" O.K. But where does that get me?" The legs of his chair scraped suddenly on the floor. " Look, I'd marry her. I want to marry her. Mrs. Allart, you've got that, haven't you? Though heaven help the poor girl who married me."

" Or heaven help the poor man who married Diana?"

He laughed. " I'll take the risk. Seriously, what do you think my chances are?"

" I don't know. I really don't know. You'll have to ask her. You'll have to talk to Diana."

" All right," he said ; it was a little as if he had been rebuffed. Then, " Still, you've got to *see* someone even to propose to them. For the half-a-dozenth time."

After that, we began to look for things to say to each other.

As we were leaving, he asked, " Are you doing anything interesting with the rest of the week-end?"

" We're going to Cley House to-morrow." ' You ' now had become practically a dual entity.

" What is Cley House?"

" It's a country house ; quite near my aunt. The gardens are wonderful—especially in September."

" You and your aunt?"

172

" Diana and——"

" Oh." He bit at his lip. " Hell. Well, anyway, the gardens must be better than what's on at the Rialto."

When I returned home to the flat, and saw her again, I learnt that he had asked her to go to the pictures with him, and she had told him she had to work.

" It seemed easiest," she said.

We sat facing each other before the fire she had lit though it was late ; our first Autumn fire. I was almost overwhelmingly thankful to be once more with her. My feeling of distaste, almost of personal meanness, at the deception that was taking place had grown wretchedly that day. It was as if only with her, any more, was I at all real.

" It isn't usually ; the easiest."

" Judith ! "

" I'm not being sanctimonious, darling—just *practical*, really."

" Was he angry ? "

" No ; he wasn't angry." (All the same, quite soon afterwards, he went back to the Paley factory in Lincoln. She wasn't surprised by this.)

She said now, " Anyway, that will probably be that, so far as he's concerned. He'll think I'm just tired of him, and he isn't the kind of person to go on and on, not if he thinks I've got tired of him. He's too, oh, I don't know—positive. It's best, really. Though I haven't. I wish I could explain to him. I don't feel any different from what I always did."

I was silent.

" Except that I know now there's something better.

173

Better for me." She paused. " Oh, what's the good of talking about it ? Even if I could : to anyone but you."

I went over to her then, and sat on the arm of her chair. " So don't let's talk about it. We can't alter anything. What was your film man like ? Did he want to make love to you ? "

" No. No, now I come to think of it, he didn't. From to-morrow I will start being attractive to men."

" Did he want your autograph ? "

Suddenly she laughed. " Well, yes," she said, " as a matter of fact he did. On the flyleaf. Apparently it's a precaution he always takes."

The next evening we had supper with my aunt in the cool Sunday evening of her dining-room. It was the only time we saw her together after our relationship had become what it was. There is something rather difficult and strange, anyway, about coming from the private intimacy of a love affair out into ordinary social contact. In our case, with my aunt, it was like very decorously wearing a paper dress. She, in a brown costume, was decorous in return. As always.

But she said twice she was pleased to see me ; that it was too long since I had been. Exceptionally, she offered us drinks.

She had bought a television she never watched, and this she put on for our amusement.

As we were watching the play, just once Diana looked at me, from across the room.

I don't know why, I can't explain quite why, but it was this particular look, and the heightened feeling it gave me of unity with her, a feeling vivid against my

174

sense of separateness from everyone else, that really brought home to me just how much I was making a life-line of her.

She was everything.

Despite our happiness, then, our joy in each other, I experienced a deep thrust of alarm that came from this knowledge of my complete vulnerability and went deep.

I remember that for the first time that night, I asked her if she would always love me.

Though she said yes, for the next day or two I consciously concentrated on work, did more than was necessary. This didn't lessen my love, but it gave me less opportunity for an obsession.

She said, " You're lucky to have something to care about the way you care about the Channing. In a way it must a bit *insulate* you."

I knew that Julian was back in London.

Then he asked me to meet him.

9

He said, seeming to look at a point just above my eyes, " I hoped it was an episode, something unaccountable on the spur of the moment you'd have finished with almost as soon as it happened. I can't tell you how much I hoped that."

I didn't answer. Our long familiarity might never have been.

" But that isn't it ; is it ? She's living with you.

175

You and she—" He stopped. One of his hands, nice hands, the fingers square at the ends, had begun to move up and down against a lapel of his jacket as if he was quite unaware of it; mechanically, pointlessly. The hand didn't seem to belong to anyone I knew. The suit, formal, double-breasted, was a familiar one being worn by a stranger. "Judith," he said, "this is intolerable for both of us. Never in the worst sort of nightmare could I have imagined anything I would have hated more. Believe me, I would have avoided it if I could; if I could have even half persuaded myself there was nothing I had to do. But I couldn't. I tried, and I couldn't. And now I can only ask you to forgive me if I say what I mean without attempting to be delicate. Because how else can I make you understand my position?"

I waited.

" It seems," he said, so that I could just hear him, " you and she have simply accepted that you should corrupt each other absolutely. In the most fundamental and vital sense."

" Whatever we have accepted, it is only between the two of us."

" But nothing is that. Nothing is ever ' only between the two of us '."

Some phrase came into my mind about our being members one of another, and he added, " Just as nothing evil can ever be ' no concern of ours '."

I suppose I might have known already that I was wasting my time, but I asked, " Only who is to decide what is evil ? Decide it finally and with certainty ? "

176

" For fear I mayn't say God to you, in this case society. Society has always seen perversion for what it is. Or if it hasn't, if the truth has been obscured, the consequences have always spoken for themselves." His eyes suddenly met mine. For the first time, we really confronted each other. " The thing is evil ; it is entirely evil ! " he said. And though the emphasis was to convince me, unmistakably it came from the depths of his own conviction. " Perhaps you can't see it as that now. Perhaps you are too near it. But don't let yourself be deluded. Don't do that with your life."

" It is too easy to say these things, just to stand there and say them."

" It is desperately hard for me to say them. An impossible rôle. It is desperately hard for me to say to you, when I'm not a priest and it isn't my job "— something new now had begun to come into his voice, something that can come, recognisably, into the voices of people about to speak of what is above, or outside, the merely rational—" that you have a soul."

Before his tone, I was silent.

" Your soul is what matters."

" Whether it should or not, my heart matters—to me."

We were no longer directly face to face.

" It isn't possible," I said then, " to ask of people that they should voluntarily give up love. Live quite without it. It is too much to ask."

" What you are doing with this girl isn't love ! Love is creative ; its very essence is life."

" The love we are talking of is human affection together with human——"

His hand all at once became motionless, was returned to his side. He seemed not to have heard me. " What you are doing isn't even just an omission or a failure. It is a positive, a grotesque denial."

" And if there is no question of choice ? "

" There are certain things as human beings we are obliged to choose—or not to choose."

Of course, that should have ended it ; but the useless exchanges persisted, with spasms of renewed feeling, like a living body reluctant to die. He said, " How can I leave you to this any more than I could leave you to drown, just pass by and leave you ? "

Pass by on the other side . . .

" Or, Judith, leave you to drown her ? She is what——"

" If you interfere, it will make nothing better but only everything much worse."

" I cannot believe it is interfering, to attempt to prevent a disaster if the chance is there. A disaster for both of you."

" If you do what you say, you will cause the disaster, not prevent it. For heaven's sake—whether you are right or wrong, surely when morality causes more distress than it saves doesn't the whole point of it become lost ? "

" Anything is better than that the two of you should live your lives like this. It is a destructive relationship," he said, " dark and destructive. Socially more destructive than a hydrogen bomb."

" Oh, no ! "

But he believed it, he believed it uncompromisingly. It would have made no difference if I had said, for instance, psychiatrists had come to believe homosexuality remains at some given per cent regardless of prevailing attitudes—or punishments.

He said, " Socially and personally."

And he left me as he had met me, with the intention of telling Andrew what he knew : if Diana and I didn't part.

" He *will* do it ? " she asked, at first as if she hadn't completely accepted what I had told her. " You said——"

" I was quite wrong. I took into account his character, but not his conscience. One's conscience will do anything. Yes, he'll do it. And Andrew, of course, will believe him."

" It's hardly a thing someone would make up ; least of all Julian."

" Besides, the truth looks so like the truth—when you know it. Even, in the end, when you don't know it."

" This will. Perhaps," she said at last, " I had better tell Andrew myself."

" What will you tell him ? That women sometimes fall in love with women, which he will know already ? That you and I have ?—which, however you tell him, will have heaven knows what effect on him."

" I could tell him that to ask me to stop loving you now would be like asking me to go abroad and stop ever having been English. And that it would be taking away from me something I never hoped to have, something——" The words came to an end on an emotional note she hadn't intended. " I know : Andrew," she said. " Can I really imagine saying that to Andrew ?

No, I can't. Well, what do *you* think we had better do ?
What will you do ? "
    " Nothing."
    " Because we don't have to do anything? Because
we aren't children or criminals and aren't answerable
to Andrew—or anyone ? "
    " Darling, not even that. To Julian, we are.
Criminals and sinners."
    " His conception of sin is too neat at the edges."
    I shrugged. " Not for any reason. Just because
there's nothing *to* do."
    What Andrew did was to ask Mrs. Quendon to come
home.

10

I had refused to be sent for ; it was from across my own
room that she said, " Mrs. Allart, I have no idea how
one behaves in such a situation as this. There is nothing
in my life that could possibly guide me. I would like
to make my visit as short as I can." After offering me
a cigarette, she put one herself into a holder. " What
I have heard about your friendship with my daughter
I dare say has been ridiculously exaggerated. I'm past
the age for believing everything I'm told. But even so
I don't pretend the whole friendship isn't quite beyond
my understanding. I've no wish to go into it. I simply
want to ask Diana to come back to my brother's with
me. That, after all, is what matters."

180

It might as well have been her room. From the first moment of seeing her I knew I hadn't the smallest chance of meeting her on any sort of equal terms.

She didn't display anger, or even the dislike one might feel for somebody one discovers has disagreeable personal habits. Perhaps she gave the impression of being disturbed. But more than anything else, I think, she was fundamentally impatient, though she softened it in social charm—which she deployed as if it were an armed force. I mean impatient at having to turn from her own grown-up life to deal with something appearing to her, irredeemably, and in spite of everything, merely silly, a pointless, incomprehensible silliness; like the silliness indulged in by children. I think she would have had more time for an illegitimate baby; at any rate she would have had more patience with its cause.

She was a very young, very feminine forty-five. Her clothes were smart and just escaped being frilly. She had Diana's face. I remember every word and every movement of her presence in my flat. I am not physically brave, but I felt I would have preferred a physical torture.

She said, " What matters is that Diana shouldn't be behaving in this way. Everything else apart, she's twenty. We are agreed about that ? " And when I didn't answer, she said, " I wonder *you* find it worth your while." Her look took me in ; a penetrating, feminine, unhostile look. She could have added, ' What's wrong with you, that you can't get yourself a man ? '

She had every advantage. She was sure she could get a man whenever she wanted to. She despised any

181

inability to do so. She was Diana's mother. She looked like Diana. She was armoured in good intentions —and basic impatience with us both.

She turned to her daughter.

" It seems a long way to have had to come, darling, to tell you one doesn't wear a gym-slip for ever."

" I'm not wearing a gym-slip." It was said very quickly.

" Then what do you imagine you *are* doing? "

" I love Judith."

There was the slightest pause. Mrs. Quendon moved in her chair. " What you are doing is being very silly." The smile was sudden : unexpected, and charming. It was intimate ; and had in it all the loitering authority, the potency, of a mother who has always, easily, been loved. It was a protest, and a private tenderness. It excluded me. " You are not for Mrs. Allart's amusement."

" I'm not amusing myself, Mrs. Quendon."

She disregarded this.

Diana said nothing, and watched, I think with a kind of pain, as her mother's intimacy was withdrawn.

Mrs. Quendon took a breath. " This is the sort of thing that should have been got over years ago, if at all. With one of your school-mistresses. You've left it too late, and you are making far too much of it. I suppose you don't see the rest of your life in exclusive terms of Mrs. Allart? "

" I can't talk to you while you are being like this."

" Then how do you expect me to be? I've said I don't know how I should be behaving. I can't carry

182

on like Andrew—behave as if you were on the streets instead of involved in some foolish infatuation for another woman. I simply don't know what to make of you. Diana, *really*—show a little sense ; a little common sense ! Say good-bye to Mrs. Allart, it's no more than she must expect, and let's see if we can't find you something at any rate to improve on this girlish situation." She added, " Now that I'm here."

" I'm sorry they bothered you. It wasn't my idea. But I can't leave Judith. I would try to explain, if you would try to understand."

Mrs. Quendon looked at her daughter for a long time, as if expecting her to waver—then she stood up. " I'm quite certain I would never understand," she said. " There are some things no-one like me could possibly understand. But I can't drag you home by the hair ; can I ? There's nothing I can do. Except say I'm sorry you're apparently capable of being so—oh, never mind. You know as well as I do what nonsense it all is. But if you're determined, what is there to do ? Only leave you to grow out of it." She picked up her gloves. " When you do, of course, you'll be sorry you insisted on wasting more time than you need have done on somebody whose attitude to life, to say the least of it, seems to be abnormally immature."

I glanced at Diana. She looked, I thought, as if she had been experiencing something quite unbearable ; something that had turned out worse, even, than she had been prepared for.

She was watching her mother.

Mrs. Quendon didn't say anything further to her.

183

To me, she said, "Your own life, of course, is your own affair. And there is no way I could interfere with it, even if I wished to. You aren't being a great help to Diana's life, however. You aren't breaking any laws that I know of, I can't call for a policeman; there's very little I *can* do. But I wonder if you've really stopped to consider. You aren't being any help to Diana at all."

She wouldn't look at Diana.

I think she cared. Despite her impatience, despite her refusal to make a scene, I think she did. It might have been her highest card: cutting herself off only to open her arms when her daughter, who loved her, was all the more ready to run into them. I don't know.

After she had gone, Diana said, "It was awful. Oh, Judith, it was awful. It was awful for you."

"I don't think we were expected to enjoy it."

"They talk about the social implications of seduction. I can't think why. Heavens, no-one would ever *choose* this. They might try it, but they wouldn't choose it." She paused. "How on earth are you going to go on working with Andrew?"

"I'm beginning to think one can do almost anything; when one has to. He could hardly be expected to resign."

"*You* could hardly be expected to. At least there's that—it's a personal thing. It's a purely personal thing." Then suddenly she said, in a different voice, "I don't want to stay in; not just stay in, the rest of the evening. Do you?"

"What do you want to do?"

184

"Anything. We could go to The Walnut. At least it would be noisy."

"Darling—I'm sorry about your mother. I'm so sorry."

"Let's stop thinking about any of it."

We had something or other to drink at The Walnut, and sandwiches we mostly left. On our way there we passed Pat's house ; her friend Pat.

"It'll be funny if we see her." She was set now on talking about something different. "Someone she knows in the Air Force is on leave. They're going dancing. He wants her to marry him." She flicked at her lighter. "She thinks she might. She quite likes him. Besides, she wants to be called ' Mrs.' "

"Do *you* ? " (But I know that I shouldn't.)

"Oh, I suppose so. Isn't vanity the main motive ? Not more than anything else. I don't want it more——"

"What ?—more than anything else."

"Nothing. You."

I looked at her.

But she didn't return my look. It was the kind of thing now I was ready to notice. With unnecessary, fastidious concentration, she removed a fragment of tobacco from her lip.

The traffic lights changed.

There was no-one we knew at the club.

Esther smiled at us from behind the bar.

One of those coincidences that do happen happened : Otto was singing the same song. ' This affair,' he sang in his honey voice, ' never will go so well——'

"I'd like to dance."

" Alas."

She ignored the remark, and my tone. She said,
" I'm writing an article for *The Observer*. On Colette."

" Tell me about it."

We talked about *The Observer*, and Colette.

At home, she kissed me with a rather desperate passion
that awoke mine.

People staying the whole night in each other's arms I
had supposed until then a pretty fiction ; that night we
did. But I felt from hour to hour she was thinking of
to-morrow.

The next day Andrew telephoned.

" He wants me to go there. His cold's worse. My
mother's there." She hesitated. " She'll be there for
lunch. I can't not ever see my mother."

" No. Diana, do you want to finish it ? Finish
with me, I mean. I——"

" No," she said. " No."

Part Three

I

"The worst things that happen to us," Martin said, months later, "we stand and wait for."

"But only because it's the worse things there's noth-ing to be done about; or if there is, we don't know what."

He had been talking about our marriage. There is a stage one can reach in hot, airless restaurants where one's consciousness of oneself and one's relations with others is planed down to an unresisting surface, and conversation runs anywhere. Or seems to do this; perhaps in reality it is drawn towards certain magnetic points.

He said, "However, it's all the past. If anything is ever 'the past'."

It was terribly hot, like being cocooned in a round bracket of white tablecloths and wine bottles. Outside it had been Spring, a new, cruel, searching Spring which had turned into the slate of a March evening, and then into darkness. A club pianist somewhere quite near was beginning his wandering, sentimental preliminary of tunes.

I didn't so much decide that evening to tell Martin about Diana, and about me, as do it because the circumstances were what they were and the opportunity all at once lay before me; was put, ready-made, before me.

He had said I would still be a part of his life, of his

190

present life, if I went to New Zealand and he never heard from me again. And I had thought : yet in a way I am farther from you *now* than the other side of the world. Because I have never offered you the truth, you of all people, and you have never taken it from me ; no part of it. I thought of Julian, and Mrs. Quendon, and Andrew—and wondered suddenly, finding I longed for his sympathy, the comfort of his male sympathy, what he would be like ; what he, Martin, who loved me, would be like if he knew.

I had thought of Andrew . . .

In the days immediately after Julian had gone to him, I hadn't seen Andrew. He had been away from the office with what had been called ' a cold ', so that I had supposed this a way of avoiding me, and thought it unlike him, and half despised him for it—though only as one tries to stiffen oneself against the enemy in any way one can, with any animosity at hand. In reality, however, it must have been something nearer to pneumonia.

When at length I had seen him, after Diana was in Lincoln with her mother, he had so obviously been ill ; he was white and hoarse-voiced still, and seemed weak, and smelt of antiseptics.

But his mouth was a narrow, obdurate line.

He stood there, short, less fat, expensively dressed, the business man who had been my father's friend, his brushed-back hair quite black, the face beneath it appearing paler than ever, and looked at me as at a card-sharper, a syphilitic card-sharper, by whom he had been personally cheated.

191

I don't exaggerate. It may seem so ; but I remember him and the way he looked too well. The way he looked when he came to my office, the words he used to underline his look : ' There's nothing I want to say to you now. Except that if you were a man I'd say plenty.'

That was almost funny. If I were a man. Not that I was disposed to laugh. So far as he was concerned I'd become . . .

Telling Martin, I didn't know how to put what for Andrew I had become.

" ' Twisted creature ' is an expression I've heard used." In the moments when he first knew the truth about me—about his wife—Martin's desire was, must have been, to inflict pain.

But earlier, when all this had started, when I had said I would write to him even from New Zealand, he had said with his voice personal, gentle almost, " A picture post-card of the view ? "

It had been so hot in the restaurant ; softly smoky : bemusing and flawless, smooth, like a drug—and all at once a temptation, so easy, with his voice gentle for me, to say I didn't think I would ever again send anyone a picture post-card of anywhere.

" Why ? "

Our dinner had been a long one, the rest of the story following. About Helen's card, and Julian, and Andrew —and Diana, and me.

It was with the coffee that he said, " I was never sure you were cold, only that I wasn't the right one. Maybe a cold homosexual would hardly bother," he added. " Being one. Anyway, it just isn't something I would

192

have thought of at all in connection with you. Homosexuality."

"Because I'm not like a man? But the woman who's physically half a man is something different."

Not that this was a revelation to him. It was just that I—when I wasn't a man, as he was, and didn't evoke any particular ideas of masculinity in his mind—should want a woman quarrelled with what was personally real to him ; that I should want her as he (the comparison was his) had wanted me.

He frowned.

"Oh, Martin, I'm sorry. I'm really sorry."

"If I've understood at all, isn't that much the same as saying one's sorry one's—oh, what? Rhesus negative?"

"There are other points of view."

Andrew's, for instance.

Andrew and I did our work now in what was supposed to be utterly impersonal detachment ; just polite enough for efficiency. Just. But if I was even anywhere near him his face changed. He did what he could to see I wasn't often near him.

I didn't know what Andrew had said when he asked Diana to go and see her mother ; or what was said when she was there. I simply knew she had been made to change her mind. I supposed by her mother.

She loves her mother, I told Martin.

"Didn't she love you?"

I shrugged. "But, anyway, after all, it was so much more comfortable to decide in the end her mother was right."

"*Andrew* must have felt pretty strongly, getting her mother back from America."

" Money's no object, of course. No doubt he's satisfied with his return."

" You don't have to talk like this, or pretend to me. I know that if I said the wrong things now I could make you cry."

Perhaps. But after months ; and because of his sympathy.

There had been no tears when she had come back from ' Four Winds '. At first there had been no reason for tears. She had been quiet, uncommunicative ; that was all. Involved in her own thoughts, but not changed in her attitude. She had wanted to make me some soup before we went to bed, and had left it too long, so that it got burnt, and she had said I couldn't rely on her for anything. But later, she had said, " I love you. I do love you."

The next morning, though, was the last morning : no doubt why the details of it remain so clear. The pink dressing-gown on the bathroom floor, smelling of her scent when I picked it up. The smile because, exceptionally, I took her tea in bed. Her decision to go early to the library and find out some things she wanted to know about Colette.

The memory of her as she went, wearing a pink beige suit, looking very dark, very young, and slim, and, oh, I don't know what word, except feminine ; pausing a moment to glance at a letter lying in the hall, not troubling to read it, but putting it in her bag, and turning round to me to say good-bye again.

When she had returned to the flat it had been to say she couldn't go on with me ; that she had been thinking

194

(trite, lethal words) and for the first time really begun to see everything it would mean. That, after all, she couldn't face such a future.

She hadn't cried ; and for me at first it had been above all a matter of trying to absorb out of sight just long enough what I had experienced before, and perhaps half expected again, but found when it came to it, when it came to losing her, I hadn't been able to prepare for ; couldn't in the least defend myself against.

I remembered—with Martin—what I had said ; the fear that explaining might go on to where it broke up altogether such as there was of my control. 'All right. It's all right. I understand. Only leave it ; just leave it.'

Then afterwards it hadn't been, really, a question of tears.

I don't know but I have wondered if homosexuals, in the nature of things, are especially prone to states of complete despair. Not, I suppose, that such reflections are very profitable.

My despair after Diana had broken up our love affair, marriage, whatever it is to be called, went beyond the losing of a loved person ; even that. It was a black, nihilistic hopelessness constituting an attitude to life itself. Nothing escaped it ; no most impersonal previous pleasure : sunlight, the smell of food, the sound, unexpectedly, of music, the sky in the small hours. There was nothing not meaningless to me, and tragic.

Suicide would have been logical—as it has seemed logical to other people, the inverted in more than their fair numbers, perhaps. Death might not have had

195

any great appeal, but certainly it didn't appeal less than living. Nor, any longer, was I capable of the feeling that to commit suicide, after all, was a kind of human defection, betrayal.

That I didn't do so was only, it seemed to me, because of the Channing. The Channing was my concern, my direct responsibility—outside anything I might or might not feel myself. It wasn't for leaving to Andrew ; or anyone. It barred the way rather as a child, I suppose, a dependent person, might have barred it : automatically.

I got over not wanting to live, got over the worst of it, then. But there were occasions still when my only object, the old object, was not to know or feel or care. I tried drinking. It didn't work. It never worked. For some reason it was simply something I couldn't do. So I would just go to bed, and lie in the dark. In the dark let me lie, alone and for ever, to mark time with— what ? Sorrow ? What was it ? I don't remember. They aren't my words, are from a poem she wrote, much later. Diana wrote.

Diana had been almost something separate. Remembering, it was confused, like a long illness, seemed without any clear divisions of time, the process of getting to where only desire for her was left, no other emotion—and in the end only a flat, undetailed desire which had got through obsessively wanting the soft, matt hair at her neck, her glad body and the white nylon, the frowning smile, things that had led the way into loving her as a person, irrecoverably, I believed, I believe, and become just the final blank emotional state of being without her.

That was the best I could achieve. I needn't have

196

bothered, trying to tell myself there was no justification for all I felt ; when has passion listened to reason ? But by contrast it seemed a matter for thankfulness.

Martin tipped his glass, and stared a moment at the light-shot, dancing white contents. " There was nothing new had cropped up ? " he asked at last. " I mean, after she saw her mother."

" What ' new ' ? And the old reasons are good enough. Believe me." Then I wished I hadn't said that. It seemed like a bid for pity. Not that pity is often what one seeks ; just comprehension. " It didn't matter, anyway. If anything at all, or anybody, could change her about me it simply didn't matter what or who."

" So you didn't even try to stop her ? "

I was half answering myself. " All I've ever had on my side was if she wanted and needed overwhelmingly to be with me."

I was glad of the silence, the respite, in which I finished my drink before he said it was strange that while I was sitting there thinking of Diana he should feel now so much closer to me.

We went on after this to the point where I was agreeing with him that psychiatry should at least be given a chance. I agreed, meaning it, since he was so decided, that I should go to a psychiatrist—though soon I would be thirty, and knew, was sure I knew, it would have been all the same at twenty. Though none of it was very real ; had more than an abstract, textbook reality.

Martin was real.

Julian and I were on speaking terms. That was all, for I could neither bear his charity, his wish to help me, which continued, unrelated to the end of any personal interest in me, nor forgive him for what he had done. However, it was enough for him to have told me about Diana.

Diana and I hadn't seen each other since she had left our flat, ludicrously and heart-breakingly taking away her things in a taxi. He told me she was marrying Gerry Paley.

" The wedding's to be at the Paleys' place, apparently. Mrs. Quendon went back to America some time ago."

He told me the news kindly.

I could find nothing to say.

I was with my aunt in Edinburgh when they were married. I saw a photograph of the wedding. Gerry looked pleased. Diana was smiling. Andrew wasn't there. It wasn't until later I heard they had gone to live somewhere outside Reigate.

The telegram came from Reigate. It was waiting for me one Saturday, after I had spent the morning at the Channing looking through a mass of summer mortgage applications. The Channing was no longer a physical refuge. I don't know how much it was an emotional one. But it was something. My father's ideal, left to me, of a big but personal and humane business was something. And in a sense, now, everything.

It was like her, sending a telegram.

Her words, pasted lifelessly across the form, were like her, and took me unawares. I felt a rush of anger that at a level of feeling I didn't control they made it impossible for me, still, to disregard them ; anger, or what passes for anger when the harsh core of sexual longing isn't melted, dissolved at length into gentleness. For though I would have given anything, everything, not to have been abandoned by her, after her marriage it had seemed to me I had arrived at last at any rate at some sort of acceptance ; some sort of self-possession. The words were : ' It is the only thing I will ever ask you again I promise but please come and see me it is so desperately important.'

I tore the telegram up.

And when I went to her it was as if I didn't love her.

But on the back of a letter in my bag, so as not possibly to be forgotten, was her address.

The letter, potent, perfumed now, still unanswered, was Martin's. It said, and had made me ashamed :

' Sometimes the truth helps and sometimes it doesn't. I think it would help us. I think it might be easier to be nicer now. I would try to be. Adjustments and compromises might be easier. For one thing there's no longer the other man—altogether more effectual than me—I supposed you should have married. And for another there is the fact that any amount of natural sexual compatibility can only be one of the satisfactions adults look for when they marry. I don't belittle it, but most of the others, now, I can only imagine from you.

199

'All the same don't misunderstand me. Don't feel uncomfortably that you are having me thrown on your mercy. I dare say men are half cut out to be bachelors anyway. It just so happens that there has always been something in you to incline me more towards the problems of marriage than the problems of being a bachelor.

'I am not indulging in myopic sentiment, either. I know it's very likely you won't change, that you have to live your life as you are. I don't even underestimate the difference there must be between us, when what I feel for you, after all, is based on ordinary sex attraction. But I love you very much in a great many ways. I miss you in a great many ways. And if there is any chance now that you might be happier married to me again, dear Judith, I would like to try.

She had given me her address, but I didn't know where it was, and stopped twice to ask for directions. Later that day I was to be reminded of the man I asked who mentioned 'The Four Bells', a pub on a corner.

The house had been newly built, at the end of an unadopted road.

She was so the same. She was wearing a dress I remembered her buying. Her dark hair, as it had always done, broke its simple, sophisticated line on the upturned collar. She had laughed one evening when she came home to the flat, and said of the black suède shoes (going back almost to our first meeting), the same shoes with their very high heels, *they* were a calculated risk, too— that had to come off. I remembered the incident,

200

in a kind of mental aside. Only her mouth seemed to me to have changed, and that because I knew all of her so precisely, intimately ; that so indefinitely I couldn't be sure, not sure the expression lines lipsticked in were harder and more than months older.

I thought, the first moment at the door, she was going to touch me ; but she only invited me in.

She was alone. I don't recall the room where we sat except, vaguely, that there were pink curtains, and pink whorls of pattern on the carpet. At first she was very polite, almost socially polite, and poised ; but it was useless, ridiculous. There are no neat, calm mechanical conventions of speech for two people who have had a love relationship, and not recovered from it. ' How are you ? ' ' You found your way.' And abruptly, in an atmosphere of besieging tension, the effort collapsed.

She raised her arm an instant against her forehead, dragging her dress—the gesture as if it had been made in weariness, or to protect herself ; personal, unguarded.

We sat facing each other : no longer visitor and visited, hostess and guest.

" Help me," she said.

" Why have you asked me to come ? "

" Because I wanted to talk to you. Because I had to. And when I did, when I did ask you, it seemed the only thing that mattered. It still seems the only thing."

I waited.

" It's about us."

" About Gerry and you ? Then surely I am the last person."

201

"Not about Gerry and me."

"I don't understand what you mean."

"Judith——"

I didn't answer.

After an instant of looking at me then, she got up and went over to the window, where some packets of cigarettes were lying in a pile on the ledge. She picked up a packet and began playing with the flap.

I wanted her to stop because of the familiarity of it; was afraid, all at once mortally afraid, of anything that could open up a way to the crumbling edge I had found still lay in wait for me. I didn't know what she was going to say. Held on to my anger, anger that she shouldn't now have left me alone; anger that in spite of all that had happened, all I could do, I should still be caught up in love for her, in dependence and desire. Listened with a part of my mind—attempting to put the distraction between us—to the mutter of traffic which came from behind the house: the interruption of gear changes, the occasional horn.

I couldn't not look at her.

She said, "All right. All right then: Gerry and me. We've quarrelled. Before I sent the telegram to you. I've never seen him like he was this morning. He doesn't lose his temper with me." She had taken a cigarette. "It was over having a baby." When she inhaled she might have been a much older woman, really needing the nicotine. "He's gone off, I've no idea where; or what he'll do. I had to see you."

I felt my throat tighten.

Was she saying Gerry had left her?

"He'll come back," she said. "I know that. But when he does I shall tell him I'm going to leave him."

In the silence, her breath of smoke cleared.

The interminable, interminable silence.

"Diana, listen. I didn't want to come here. I didn't want to see you again. I came because—no, I don't know why I came. But not to talk to you about your marriage."

Quickly she asked, "Then who am I to talk to?" Her expression had altered. "Gerry? It might as well be in Arabic. If I tried to explain to Gerry. If I tried to tell him the truth why I can't have his baby; why I've got to leave him." She paused. "He wants me to have a baby. He wants a son. And he's decided I *need* one. That women do, just as soon as they're safely married. He's beautifully conventional in his ideas. And unimaginative : when he's still very much at the stage, I assure you, of preferring his wife a convenient shape."

I turned away at this, and she added, "Not that he hasn't had a good go. I've let him do whatever he wanted."

It was these words, the world they called up, that sharpened everything I had against the past into hot, goading stabs on my feeling for her. I said, it must have been nice for him.

"It hasn't been nice for me."

"Why did you marry him?"

"Because I had to do something," she said. "If I wasn't to end up with a parrot and a couple of cats. Because he was there. Because he asked me."

203

" They aren't reasons."

" Then because it was a way to tell Andrew to go to hell. Is that a reason? Because it was the only way. Along with giving back to him his too-big ring. So much for Andrew's caring about me." She threw her cigarette butt into the grate. I paid no attention to why she was talking like this about Andrew. It didn't seem to matter. " What do you want me to say? Apparently it had to be a man. 'For all concerned.' What difference did it make *what* man? "

Oh, I was glad of my anger. " To Gerry? "

" He wanted me. He always has. He'd have wanted me anyway. Well, what should I have done? "

' Stayed with me,' I thought; stayed with me as I would have stayed with you in spite of anything it cost me. And perhaps for the first time I let the bitterness of the thought remain undiluted by reason; let it luxuriously expand, untrammelled by reason. " Not married Gerry. You saw what happened with Martin and me. You'd seen. You *knew*."

" I knew I was a homosexual."

" You knew you would never love Gerry."

I doubt if one can ever be quite sure of one's own motives. I am sure that I feared any further involvement with her, feared desperately any return to the worst of what was past. And if I didn't know then I *felt* anger was my best chance against it. Anger over Gerry was there at hand. An immaculate reinforcement. All at once I cared bitterly about Gerry. Whether at heart it was for me or for him, I am not sure.

She looked at me. " I knew I was a homosexual,"

204

she said again.   Colour had begun touching the whiteness of her face.   " I expect you did me a good turn showing me.   I expect it's as well to know—if you aren't very good at living any other way.   What I didn't know was that I wasn't tougher.   I didn't imagine I'd ever want Gerry.   I didn't imagine anything.   I just thought I could manage."

" How could you manage ?   How could either of you manage ?   When——"

" I might have done.   If it hadn't been for you."

" ' If it hadn't been for ' is senseless.   It's senseless. You did live with me, and love me, and decide you'd had enough of it, and decide to change it for Gerry."

" It wasn't like that."

" Then what was it like ?   You didn't have to go." She swallowed, as if she might say something.   " And when you did, when you did go to him, whatever else it was it was—cheating."

The streets-away traffic muttered by.

" So all right," she said.   Her voice was harder, harder-edged, than I had known it.   She stood in front of me, trembling.   Her face now was set, her mouth hard, hostile :   the mouth, mauve-pink beneath its lipstick, I had kissed ;   and Gerry had.   " If you're determined to quarrel with me—all right.   I didn't mean it to be like this.   It wasn't going to be like this at all.   But if you don't love me, now ;   if you're determined to quarrel——"   She shrugged, and I clung to my silence.   " I've got quite good at it after this morning. Only don't mix me up with your own conscience.   I haven't cheated.   I never pretended to Gerry I felt the

205

way he does. If he thought I'd change it was his idea : it was never part of the bargain. You needn't bother worrying about Gerry. He's had his money's worth."

He's had his money's worth. Oh, God. "Like paying a prostitute ? "

" Like going into it with his flies open."

" That's——"

" Crude."

" A stupid way of putting it. What did you expect ? He wouldn't want to make love to——? "

" Well, I feel crude." Her voice rose sharply above mine. " And since you're here I'll tell you how crude I feel. I feel like saying just once to someone, I can't endure it any more when he does what you call making love to me. I can't endure being pushed back on the bed as if he's sure it's what really I'm dying for ; what every woman is, and if I don't seem eager I'm just being coy. Though how would he like having to make love, oh, to Martin ? I wait for it, and dread it, and almost suggest it to get it over ; and start hating him. And I hate the hard bits on his oh so athletic fingers, and the unending hair, and the way he sniffs and drips all self-respecting male in his manly, manly nakedness. And I wouldn't hate him if I didn't have to keep going to bed with him."

I stood up ; I couldn't listen to it any more. But she caught hold of me, hurting my arm. " When it's something quite different I long for. You *will* listen. Only I can't go on with it. I can't have his baby, because I can't——"

" Because you can't think of anyone else for even an

instant?" Suddenly I was standing shouting at her. "Well, why should I disagree with you? I have no reason——"

"How much did anyone think of me? How much did I get of the things I wanted? How much did they let me have?"

"You chose. I have no reason to disagree. You chose. You could have stayed with me. I know everything I said, but you'd left it too late; what I'd said at first didn't mean anything any longer. You let me love you. I loved you. I *loved* you. More than anyone I ever had. It was the worst thing that could have happened in my life." I pushed her away from me. "But it's finished. And now there's Gerry. What are you going to do to Gerry? You married him when you should never have done; you wouldn't give him a chance to get on without you. You've used him. And now, what are you going to do? Is the idea that he should be just a casual victim of our intolerable, wretched mess? When the least, the very least, you can do is——"

"Give him the baby we'd never have?"

At the words, the dreadful words, cried out as they were, all my resentful hostility towards her dropped steeply away; dropped away for the substitute, unnatural thing it was. And in the long moments that followed there was only pity for her, and love.

She had sat down. She sat very still.

At last she said, "Do you want to wait and see Gerry? He won't be seeing Andrew. Any more than I do. See him."

207

" No.   I'll——"

" Because I shall stay with him, if he wants me.   I
love you.   And I wanted to come back to you.   I
wanted to ask you if I could.   But that isn't the way
it's going to work out, is it?   And I'll have his baby.
Which, in spite of all you've said "—she gave me then
the merest frowning trace, travesty of a smile—" is
more than you can say of Martin."

It seemed that only good-bye remained.

We had reached the front door before she added,
" That *can't* be the last thing I ever say to you.   Judith.
There's something else.   I was going to tell you : and
I will, anyway.   Though I know it would be better
not ; and I don't know now why it matters.   But it
does.   It matters hopelessly what you think of me.
What you'll think of me for the rest of our lives.   It will
always matter "—and she told me about Andrew ;
about the day she had gone to lunch at ' Four Winds ' ;
the day he had issued his ultimatum.

" Either I finished with you, or he did," she said.
" That was the blackmail.   So it would have been all
of them.   Not just him and my mother, but Ammersgate,
Rivers, his wife, all of them.   When he said he wouldn't
work with you, it didn't mean he was the one who would
go.   He was ready to do anything to you if he had to ;
when he saw my mother wasn't.   Anything to stop us.
It would have been horrible for you.   That's what I
thought.   It would have been quite horrible.   It would
have been too much."   She avoided my stare.   " That's
what I thought at the time.   I couldn't stick to it—
but I thought it at the time.   And I knew you'd refuse

to be blackmailed ; if you heard of it. You wouldn't have just walked out of the Channing. Anyway, the Channing's yours. Andrew wrote to you, but I tore the letter up. Then I got out. And showed him the white flag."

I was still staring at her.

" It was the letter that did it. I imagined at first I was going to let them get on with it. Only I saw the letter. It didn't say much, but it was an awful letter ; it was obvious what it would be like for you, and I wasn't —well, I just didn't think I was a good enough buy. Not at that price. Not when I wouldn't ever really be much good to you."

" Diana——"

" I don't exactly come into the ' good type ' category. That must be pretty apparent by now. I can't even be relied on not to change my mind about being ' noble '." She didn't pause before going on, " And there was nothing we could do. Except holes and corners, mean, miserable holes and corners after what we'd—oh, never mind. With everything coming out just the same in the long run, the way it does. Besides, anyway, finishing it completely seemed—at the time at least—a bit less mean than weakly starting to be furtive. At the time. ' At the time ' is so terribly out of date."

I said then, " I would rather you had told me," astonished myself at the understatement.

" I should have thought it had been bad enough with Andrew as it is. And you might have interfered. You might have refused to let me save you." She made no attempt to keep the self-derision from her voice.

209

" Still, now I've told you. Because I had to. There *is* the small point that to-day I would have let anything happen to you—if only I could have you back. But still, I've told you. Now it's all too late."

We looked at each other.

A second or two passed, and the telephone rang.

When I went with her and saw Gerry, his young face was haggard and without its fresh warmth. All down one cheek was a dark, sullen bruise. Only the bright hair seemed alive. Gerry, who didn't drink, but had troubles with his wife and a conventional side to his nature, Gerry, who was made for life, and relished it, had walked out of ' The Four Bells ' across the path of a lorry, and very nearly died.

Very nearly. But not quite.

She stood by the hospital bed, silent.

I became aware of her expression to find that it was one I hadn't seen before, and couldn't with certainty interpret.

3

Afterwards, I did what I could. There wasn't much. A few practical things ; and the shelving of good-bye.

She needed me to go on seeing her—it was all we had clear between us—and so I did. Though our continued contact was like being carried on in a train which has failed, after all, to stop at one's destination :

210

not sure any longer where one is going, and making no mention of it. We had no emotional ' understanding ', now ; nothing beyond an understanding of the interim nature of our contact. We simply didn't speak of the emotional, the personal.

I felt rather than knew at that period after Gerry's accident, when she was almost fanatical in her service of his needs, when everything she did and said was a direct expression only of concern for him, that what she had experienced initially—her sense of horror, if that was it—had become in some way a living, developing part of her ; something quite different from any clear-cut, limited reaction, however intense, to a given occurrence. I couldn't explain myself better than this. I didn't know precisely what it was I meant—though I understood later. But I was as aware as if she had referred to it of the distress in her that went on almost chemically changing, *darkening* her whole being long after Gerry was out of danger and pain.

He got better ; he was young and strong. Then he was due to leave hospital and I wouldn't have seen her any more, I suppose : only there was one further thing I could do.

I had very little knowledge of the relations now existing between them, of their private marriage world, and didn't try to have more, but she had told me that he wanted them to go away together before he returned to the lab., to Norway was his idea. Which wasn't particularly easy to arrange at short notice ; not, anyway, with a car. She said it wasn't easy.

So while Gerry went on ahead with his parents to

211

Lincoln, where he and Diana were to stay a few days after he had come out of hospital, I took her to see the man I knew who had a travel agency ; the man Andrew had invited to her party.

His flat was outside London.

She asked when we met, " Is it far ? " She seemed nervous.

She was nervous—preoccupied and on edge—throughout the visit.

He said he would arrange something.

It was as we sat together in a half-empty tube train, returning to London, that for the first time since the hospital telephone call we once more spoke of ourselves. It was then that, quite suddenly, she turned to me and said, " Do you ever think of France, and the hut, and think : all this—because of that ? "

A tremor went through my body at the question. " If I do, I remind myself that women mustn't love women."

" I haven't loved ' women ' ; I've loved you."

" Perhaps it has been decided that's worse."

The wheels of the train quietened again for her to say, " People shouldn't have interfered. They should have left me to you. It's only meant débris for everyone to get cut on."

" People interfere for the best."

" There's no best. It would have been better to leave us alone. And kinder. That's all."

The station passed.

I couldn't hear the first part of what she said next. I heard "——but that's what it was. That's what I felt. For an instant when I saw him I was sorry. I was sorry, I wanted it, that he wasn't dead—and I wasn't free. That's what I've come to without you ; with trying to live as if I wasn't me at all. I wanted him to be dead."

The effect of the words at first on me was total, annihilating ; like being struck in the face.

" That's what Gerry will be taking away with him," she was saying. " That's what he has for a wife."

She faced me a moment, displaced, alone ; suggesting nothing. And turned away.

Slowly then, slowly, my sense of shock began to break down into fragments of thought ; and though often in the future it was to re-form, as the station approached where she would get out and go on to Gerry, to her life with him, and his with her, with the wife whose desire had been his death, I was thinking, no longer able to think one line of action any more ' right ' than the other : I can't. Even if you would now. I haven't the heart left for loving you. For the end of it all, or for the beginning. If we ever stood a chance, and perhaps once we might have done, some sort of chance, having so little in place of each other, we've no chance now. It's too late ; already it's all too far gone in tragedy. To try again could be only the ultimate stupidity.

Those were the things that I said to myself.

" Good-bye, Judith. Thank you. You've been kind. I don't know when I shall see you."

I sat motionless and watched her as she walked to the doors. They opened. Her heels had sounded on the wooden floor. She didn't walk any more as if conscious of her beauty. Her belt was pulled tight; it no longer reminded me she was tall.

The doors were closing as I followed her . . .

4

All that was last summer. We're living in the same flat. It's our home, after all. My aunt has gone to live in Edinburgh. Everybody knows everything now; except perhaps for what it is only possible to know through a perception of the shared nature of all loving. Helen rather sides with Julian.

They say that Gerry's drinking too much.

I've left the Channing, and am doing something else. It became, finally, a question of the least harm. Diana has finished her second book. At any rate it's true, it's true, that we love each other.

Not that I deceive myself there's immunity in that; from next summer, and the summer after.

A few of the publications of
THE NAIAD PRESS, INC.
P.O. Box 10543 • Tallahassee, Florida 32302
Phone (904) 539-9322
Mail orders welcome. Please include 15% postage.

TO THE LIGHTNING by Catherine Ennis. 208 pp. Romantic
Lesbian 'Robinson Crusoe' adventure.   ISBN 0-941483-06-1 $8.95

THE OTHER SIDE OF VENUS by Shirley Verel. 224 pp.
Luminous romantic love story.   ISBN 0-941483-07-X   8.95

MEMORY BOARD by Jane Rule. 336 pp. Memorable novel
about an aging Lesbian couple.   ISBN 0-941483-02-9   8.95

THE ALWAYS ANONYMOUS BEAST by Lauren Wright
Douglas. 224 pp. A Caitlin Reese mystery. First in a series.
     ISBN 0-941483-04-5   8.95

SEARCHING FOR SPRING by Patricia A. Murphy. 224 pp.
Novel about the recovery of love.   ISBN 0-941483-00-2   8.95

DUSTY'S QUEEN OF HEARTS DINER by Lee Lynch. 240 pp.
Romantic blue-collar novel.   ISBN 0-941483-01-0   8.95

PARENTS MATTER by Ann Muller. 240 pp. Parents'
relationships with Lesbian daughters and gay sons.
     ISBN 0-930044-91-6   9.95

THE PEARLS by Shelley Smith. 176 pp. Passion and fun in
the Caribbean sun.   ISBN 0-930044-93-2   7.95

MAGDALENA by Sarah Aldridge. 352 pp. Epic Lesbian novel
set on three continents.   ISBN 0-930044-99-1   8.95

THE BLACK AND WHITE OF IT by Ann Allen Shockley.
144 pp. Short stories.   ISBN 0-930044-96-7   7.95

SAY JESUS AND COME TO ME by Ann Allen Shockley. 288
pp. Contemporary romance.   ISBN 0-930044-98-3   8.95

LOVING HER by Ann Allen Shockley. 192 pp. Romantic love
story.   ISBN 0-930044-97-5   7.95

MURDER AT THE NIGHTWOOD BAR by Katherine V.
Forrest. 240 pp. A Kate Delafield mystery. Second in a series.
     ISBN 0-930044-92-4   8.95

ZOE'S BOOK by Gail Pass. 224 pp. Passionate, obsessive love
story.   ISBN 0-930044-95-9   7.95

WINGED DANCER by Camarin Grae. 228 pp. Erotic Lesbian
adventure story.   ISBN 0-930044-88-6   8.95

PAZ by Camarin Grae. 336 pp. Romantic Lesbian adventurer
with the power to change the world.   ISBN 0-930044-89-4   8.95

SOUL SNATCHER by Camarin Grae. 224 pp. A puzzle, an
adventure, a mystery — Lesbian romance.   ISBN 0-930044-90-8   8.95

THE LOVE OF GOOD WOMEN by Isabel Miller. 224 pp.
Long-awaited new novel by the author of the beloved *Patience
and Sarah*.   ISBN 0-930044-81-9   8.95

THE HOUSE AT PELHAM FALLS by Brenda Weathers. 240
pp. Suspenseful Lesbian ghost story.   ISBN 0-930044-79-7   7.95

HOME IN YOUR HANDS by Lee Lynch. 240 pp. More stories
from the author of *Old Dyke Tales*.   ISBN 0-930044-80-0   7.95

EACH HAND A MAP by Anita Skeen. 112 pp. Real-life poems
that touch us all.   ISBN 0-930044-82-7   6.95

SURPLUS by Sylvia Stevenson. 342 pp. A classic early Lesbian
novel.   ISBN 0-930044-78-9   6.95

PEMBROKE PARK by Michelle Martin. 256 pp. Derring-do
and daring romance in Regency England.   ISBN 0-930044-77-0   7.95

THE LONG TRAIL by Penny Hayes. 248 pp. Vivid adventures
of two women in love in the old west.   ISBN 0-930044-76-2   8.95

HORIZON OF THE HEART by Shelley Smith. 192 pp. Hot
romance in summertime New England.   ISBN 0-930044-75-4   7.95

AN EMERGENCE OF GREEN by Katherine V. Forrest. 288
pp. Powerful novel of sexual discovery.   ISBN 0-930044-69-X   8.95

THE LESBIAN PERIODICALS INDEX edited by Claire
Potter. 432 pp. Author & subject index.   ISBN 0-930044-74-6   29.95

DESERT OF THE HEART by Jane Rule. 224 pp. A classic;
basis for the movie *Desert Hearts*.   ISBN 0-930044-73-8   7.95

SPRING FORWARD/FALL BACK by Sheila Ortiz Taylor.
288 pp. Literary novel of timeless love.   ISBN 0-930044-70-3   7.95

FOR KEEPS by Elisabeth Nonas. 144 pp. Contemporary novel
about losing and finding love.   ISBN 0-930044-71-1   7.95

TORCHLIGHT TO VALHALLA by Gale Wilhelm. 128 pp.
Classic novel by a great Lesbian writer.   ISBN 0-930044-68-1   7.95

LESBIAN NUNS: BREAKING SILENCE edited by Rosemary
Curb and Nancy Manahan. 432 pp. Unprecedented autobiographies
of religious life.   ISBN 0-930044-62-2   9.95

THE SWASHBUCKLER by Lee Lynch. 288 pp. Colorful novel
set in Greenwich Village in the sixties.   ISBN 0-930044-66-5   7.95

MISFORTUNE'S FRIEND by Sarah Aldridge. 320 pp. Histori-
cal Lesbian novel set on two continents.   ISBN 0-930044-67-3   7.95

A STUDIO OF ONE'S OWN by Ann Stokes. Edited by
Dolores Klaich. 128 pp. Autobiography.   ISBN 0-930044-64-9   7.95

SEX VARIANT WOMEN IN LITERATURE by Jeannette
Howard Foster. 448 pp. Literary history.   ISBN 0-930044-65-7   8.95

A HOT-EYED MODERATE by Jane Rule. 252 pp. Hard-hitting
essays on gay life; writing; art.   ISBN 0-930044-57-6   7.95

INLAND PASSAGE AND OTHER STORIES by Jane Rule.
288 pp. Wide-ranging new collection.   ISBN 0-930044-56-8   7.95

WE TOO ARE DRIFTING by Gale Wilhelm. 128 pp. Timeless
Lesbian novel, a masterpiece.   ISBN 0-930044-61-4   6.95

AMATEUR CITY by Katherine V. Forrest. 224 pp. A Kate
Delafield mystery. First in a series.   ISBN 0-930044-55-X   7.95

THE SOPHIE HOROWITZ STORY by Sarah Schulman. 176
pp. Engaging novel of madcap intrigue.   ISBN 0-930044-54-1   7.95

THE BURNTON WIDOWS by Vickie P. McConnell. 272 pp. A
Nyla Wade mystery, second in the series.   ISBN 0-930044-52-5   7.95

OLD DYKE TALES by Lee Lynch. 224 pp. Extraordinary
stories of our diverse Lesbian lives.   ISBN 0-930044-51-7   7.95

DAUGHTERS OF A CORAL DAWN by Katherine V. Forrest.
240 pp. Novel set in a Lesbian new world.   ISBN 0-930044-50-9   7.95

THE PRICE OF SALT by Claire Morgan. 288 pp. A milestone
novel, a beloved classic.   ISBN 0-930044-49-5   8.95

AGAINST THE SEASON by Jane Rule. 224 pp. Luminous,
complex novel of interrelationships.   ISBN 0-930044-48-7   7.95

LOVERS IN THE PRESENT AFTERNOON by Kathleen
Fleming. 288 pp. A novel about recovery and growth.
     ISBN 0-930044-46-0   8.95

TOOTHPICK HOUSE by Lee Lynch. 264 pp. Love between
two Lesbians of different classes.   ISBN 0-930044-45-2   7.95

MADAME AURORA by Sarah Aldridge. 256 pp. Historical
novel featuring a charismatic "seer."   ISBN 0-930044-44-4   7.95

CURIOUS WINE by Katherine V. Forrest. 176 pp. Passionate
Lesbian love story, a best-seller.   ISBN 0-930044-43-6   7.95

BLACK LESBIAN IN WHITE AMERICA by Anita Cornwell.
141 pp. Stories, essays, autobiography.   ISBN 0-930044-41-X   7.50

CONTRACT WITH THE WORLD by Jane Rule. 340 pp.
Powerful, panoramic novel of gay life.   ISBN 0-930044-28-2   7.95

YANTRAS OF WOMANLOVE by Tee A. Corinne. 64 pp.
Photos by noted Lesbian photographer.   ISBN 0-930044-30-4   6.95

MRS. PORTER'S LETTER by Vicki P. McConnell. 224 pp.
The first Nyla Wade mystery.   ISBN 0-930044-29-0   7.95

TO THE CLEVELAND STATION by Carol Anne Douglas.
192 pp. Interracial Lesbian love story.   ISBN 0-930044-27-4   6.95

THE NESTING PLACE by Sarah Aldridge. 224 pp. A
three-woman triangle—love conquers all!   ISBN 0-930044-26-6   7.95

VOLUTE BOOKS

JOURNEY TO FULFILLMENT	Early classics by Valerie	3.95
A WORLD WITHOUT MEN	Taylor: The Erika Frohmann	3.95
RETURN TO LESBOS	series.	3.95

These are just a few of the many Naiad Press titles — we are the oldest and largest lesbian/feminist publishing company in the world. Please request a complete catalog. We offer personal service; we encourage and welcome direct mail orders from individuals who have limited access to bookstores carrying our publications.